Jealous-Hearted Me

Jealous-Hearted Me

And Other Stories

by Nancy Huddleston Packer

JOHN DANIEL AND COMPANY
SANTA BARBARA / 1997

Previous publications:

"Jealous-Hearted Me" in *Southern Review*
"I Never Said a Word" in *Southwest Review*
"The Boy Friend" in *The Stanford Magazine*
"Mosquitoes" in *Epoch*
"Ecuador" in *Southwest Review*

Published by John Daniel & Company
A division of Daniel and Daniel, Publishers, Inc.
Post Office Box 21922
Santa Barbara, CA 93121

Book design: Eric Larson

LIBRARY OF CONGRESS CATALOGING-IN-PUBLICATION DATA
Packer, Nancy Huddleston.
    Jealous hearted me : stories / Nancy Huddleston Packer.
        p.   cm.
    ISBN 1-880284-20-0 (pbk. alk. paper)
    ISBN 1-880284-24-3 (cloth alk. paper)
    I. Title.
    PS3566.A318J4   1997
    813'.54—dc20   96-9621
                                                CIP

For Gloria and Bill Broder

Contents

Jealous-Hearted Me

AFTER Poppa passed on, I thought for sure Momma would come live with me and Lloyd in Montgomery. Poppa had been house-bound so long, she deserved a good time. What with my Sara a junior at the University of Montevallo and my Carl working for a big construction firm in Mobile, I could devote myself to Momma.

But she said, "I'm not going to transport my limbs and my trunk a hundred miles away from my roots to live in somebody else's dinky little back room."

"It isn't a dinky back room. Is it, Lloyd?" We have a wonderful big old house near downtown.

"Now, Jean," Lloyd said, "your momma knows what she wants." He just hates to get mixed up in it.

"If you want to live with me so bad," Momma said, in that little triumphant voice of hers, "you two can just move back to Birmingham. Plenty of nice rooms in my house."

"That'll be the day," Lloyd said. Lloyd loved Momma almost as much as I did, but of course he had his business to tend. He makes pup tents and plastic covers for toasters.

Momma tried living alone for a month, but she said she kept waking up in the middle of the night, hearing people rummaging around in the cellar. She wanted someone in the house with her. That's the way with Momma—she has to have it all her own way, no matter who is inconvenienced.

So Lloyd and I had to find her a companion, someone

grateful just to have a good home. The woman would have to be there every night, although Momma said she wouldn't mind coming to see us every once in a while, if Lloyd would pick her up when he had business in Birmingham. She said she would not ride in public conveyances, because people smelled bad and spat on the floor. Of course we would come to visit her every month as usual.

More than twenty women called about the advertisement we put in the newspaper. Momma said no to some over the telephone, claiming she knew they were ugly without seeing them, but we interviewed almost a dozen that Friday afternoon. One enormous woman all in pink—hair and skin and clothes, even a patch of dangling pink petticoat—just begged for the job. She said she was desperate. When she left, Momma said she didn't particularly want a desperado. Another woman from Oneonta had a face Lloyd said looked like a hatchet that had been used to chop cement, and she talked in a loud countrified voice. I couldn't stand that voice, Momma said. Another scratched so much we decided she'd bring fleas with her. A girl of eighteen showed up, popping her gum and winking. Just try to keep her in every night.

Toward evening a frail, pretty little woman about forty years old came knocking at the door. She said her name was Nina, and she stood with her hands clasped, a shy, timid look on her face. I thought she must have fallen on hard times, hadn't grown up in them.

"Please do come in," I said.

When Momma came down the steps, Nina stood up from the settee, and for a moment I thought she was going to curtsy. "Now, honey, you just sit right back down and let me look at you," Momma said. "Isn't she pretty, Jean?"

I said, "Yes." I decided she was so delicate she might be tubercular.

She said she was from Memphis and had come to Birmingham after she separated from her husband. She didn't have any children. She said she wasn't destitute or homeless—

she sold cosmetics at a department store in one of the suburbs, and she had a studio apartment that she could call her own even though the furniture was just ugly rented stuff. What she wanted was companionship. An acquaintance of hers who worked at the beauty parlor where Momma got her weekly shampoo and set had told her Momma was looking for someone.

"My friend says you're the sweetest woman, just so friendly, and not a bit of a snob."

It is true. Momma can be very open and friendly and gracious, and wherever she went people loved her. Grocery clerks greeted her on the street. The postman stopped to chat. Even the garbage men cried "Howyadoing, Mrs. Blaine?" as they rattled away. I didn't think it was quite right for Momma to stand at the window waving to garbage men. It seemed to me she spread her affections a little thin. I inherited Poppa's standoffishness.

"I know I'd love it here," Nina said, ducking her head and glancing through her lashes at Momma. "I mean, if you'd have me."

I said, "We've seen a lot of people today. Tomorrow morning we'll telephone the one that's best for Momma."

Momma said, "I know already who's best." She batted her eyes as if she were a teenager, and Nina batted right back. "I believe we'll make just a wonderful team. What do you think, honey?"

I thought she was talking to me, but before I could answer Nina piped in with "I do devoutly hope so." Seeing the way they looked at each other, you would have thought they were long-lost best friends.

That night I went into Momma's room. She was lying up in her four-poster with its pink-and-blue ruffles and ribbons hanging down from the top. Her hair was covered with clamps that had little teeth that make your hair wavy, and she was crocheting some little square of something, whipping the needle in and out. She was always doing handwork.

"Momma," I said, "I don't know about this Nina."

"You just met her today," she said, "and you're not too quick about people."

"I liked that woman from Oneonta," I said. "Seemed straight and honest. I know her voice was irritating, with that hillbilly clanging, but you wouldn't have to hear it much. You aren't looking for a *friend*."

"I wouldn't mind having one, though. You know how your father was those last years. He didn't much like for me to be too cozy with anyone."

"She seems sickly."

"Just because she's not a big horse."

"I am not a horse," I said. "I am a normal 18, not even a half size." I inherited my size from poppa's side. By the time I was eleven, I was bigger all around than Momma.

"My goodness, Jean, I didn't say you were a horse. I've never in my life known anybody so dag sensitive."

"I just didn't much like her," I said.

Momma laughed. "Now don't be jealous. Turn out the overhead when you leave."

"Jealous!" I said. "Why would I be jealous?"

Momma put the crochet on the bedside table and snapped off the lamp. "It's just your nature," she said.

She meant my brother Thad. He is six years older than I am, and everybody has always said he was Momma's favorite—he took after her side of the family. He is an officer in the US Army and stationed all over the world. He didn't get home very often, but did she evermore kill the fatted calf when he came. If he had wanted to pee in my ear, Momma would have held me down. And of course if *he* had wanted Momma to live with him, she would have sprouted wings to get there. Except of course his wife wouldn't have allowed it for one minute—Dinah's not easy the way Lloyd is.

Nina wasn't to come until the following Sunday. I didn't particularly want to be there when she moved in, but it was my duty to stay nights with Momma until she did. So Lloyd took the bus back to Montgomery and left me his car.

Sunday was a lovely day, the kind Alabama gets only in late May, a breeze as sweet as sugar water. After church, Momma and I sat on the front porch in the glider. About one o'clock, a taxi stopped and Nina got out.

"A taxi?" I said. "She doesn't have any friends to drive her?"

But Momma was already down the walk, calling, "Welcome, honey, welcome." They hugged each other. The taxi driver opened the trunk and set two enormous suitcases on the sidewalk. Nina paid the driver and then picked up one of the suitcases. When she reached for the other one, Momma shouldered her aside and picked it up. Nina just laughed. Of course, I ran down the walk and snatched the suitcase from Momma.

After we had worked the luggage up the stairway and into Thad's old room, I said, "Well, I guess I'll head for home." Momma didn't say a word. I asked her to walk out to the porch with me, and I whispered, "Now if things don't work out, I'm only as far away as a telephone call."

She didn't even wait for me to drive away before she was back in the house with Nina.

When I got to Montgomery, the first thing I did after giving Lloyd his hello-kiss was call Momma. When Poppa was so sick, I got in the habit of calling Momma every night. It only cost a dollar or so, and that was 365 dollars a year worth of peace of mind. I let the phone ring eleven times and still no answer. I figured they went to the store to get some groceries. But I didn't get an answer when I tried again an hour later.

By ten o'clock, I was beginning to fret. Lloyd said, "Don't be silly, Jean. You think that woman's killed her or something?"

I said, "I wouldn't be all that surprised, to tell the truth. There's something about her I don't much trust."

Momma finally answered at ten-forty-five. "Where on earth have you been?" I asked her.

"We went to dinner and the picture show," she said.

"Why," I said, you haven't been to the movies in twenty years."

"It's about time, then, isn't it?" she answered. "Did you have anything special on your mind?"

"Dr. Bill says you've been under a lot of strain and you should take it easy."

"That's not what he said," Momma answered. "He said I should have some fun. And believe me, Jean, Nina's more fun than a passel of puppies."

After that, it was just one big carnival at Momma's. I never knew Momma to be so giddy and social. Nina taught her how to play canasta, and they had canasta parties with neighbors and some of her cousins she hadn't socialized with since Poppa got sick. One night they had a bingo party for twenty people. I could hardly get Momma on the phone. The line would be busy and then she'd say call me later, and later nobody would answer. The times we talked, her whole conversation was Nina Nina Nina. Nina and I went to the picture show, Nina and I had the Crawfords over, Nina and I played canasta with Cousin Charles and his wife.

"Doesn't Nina have any friends of her own?" I asked.

"You know she's new in town, Jean, but my friends just love her to death because she's so sweet and thoughtful. Yesterday she brought me some liquid stuff from the store. It pulls your skin tight and youngs up your face. Nina says we have to get my skin looking as girlish as I feel."

"I hope you're not overdoing," I said. "People your age have to watch out."

"The thing they have to watch out for," Momma said in that little quick voice of hers, "is our daughters trying to put us in the grave before we're dead."

I knew I was going to cry, and so I just hung up the phone. It was ringing within a minute, but I wouldn't answer until it hit the third one.

"Now, listen, Jean," Momma said. "I didn't mean to hurt your feelings, but you know how you are."

"I am not how I am," I said.

"You don't need to worry about Nina," she said.

"I am not worried about anybody named Nina," I said. "I am worried about my mother. I am worried that my mother is overdoing and will pay the price."

"The price I'm paying is I feel ten years younger. Nina says I have more get-up-and-go than anyone she knows."

If she had called to apologize, she had a mighty poor way of doing it. I didn't say anything, and pretty soon I heard her calling away from the phone, "Just a minute, honey," and that was the end of the conversation.

The next Saturday Lloyd and I drove to Birmingham for our monthly visit. When we arrived, Momma and Nina were sitting at a brand new card table working a thousand-piece jigsaw puzzle, some kind of gloomy painting from old times. I never knew Momma to do such a thing before.

"My goodness," I said.

"Don't talk," she said, flapping her hand at us. "We're concentrating. We've about got it licked, haven't we, Nina?"

Lloyd sat down and to indicate he didn't mind waiting, he began cleaning his fingernails. All he does is move the dirt from under one nail to under another until he gathers a little ball, and then he flicks it away. I hate it when he does that, but he didn't look at me.

"Eureka!" Nina cried. "Here's the key piece, that Duke's face we been looking for." Momma stared at Nina as though they had discovered gold. Nina handed Momma the piece, and Momma set it in and gave a little squeal of delight. Then Nina set in a piece and then Momma and then it was Nina's turn again. They were hand over fist putting in pieces.

I said, "We have a reservation for one o'clock."

Momma sighed. "I reckon we can take a recess. But I've

got so I dearly love jigsaw puzzles."

"You never much cared for wasting time like that before," I said. "You'd be crocheting or embroidering or doing something else useful."

She laughed. "I guess this proves you *can* teach an old dog new tricks if you have the right teacher. Come on, Nina. Let's go."

I looked at Lloyd. We hadn't invited Nina. But Lloyd just inspected his fingernails.

Nina smiled at Momma in that simpering way she had and said, "Oh, Clara, I won't go. I know you want to be with your family just by yourself." Clara! Lloyd had never called her Clara once in the nearly twenty-six years he'd known her.

"Isn't she silly?" Momma said, and after a quick look at me, Lloyd agreed she sure was.

We had a really nice restaurant picked out on the top of Red Mountain, overlooking the city. When we got there I said, "I'm sure we'll have to wait—we're one more than our reservation."

But Lloyd gave the fellow a five-dollar bill and we were seated right away, at a window table. Ever the good host, Lloyd made sure he and I sat with our backs to the view.

"Now don't let that sun get on you," Momma said to Nina. "Just look at her skin, Jean. Like a baby's."

"Nice," I said. It was true. Her skin was white and soft. That was no surprise to me—she hadn't spent half of each summer picking bugs off my hydrangeas and Lloyd's roses and the other half sitting by the side of the YMCA swimming pool to make sure my children didn't drown. She had nothing to look after but that skin.

All through lunch, when Momma and Nina weren't oohing and ah-ing over the view, they were talking about this movie and that party and who said what and what they really meant. And Lloyd was laughing at everything either of them said. I didn't say a word because I didn't want Momma to say right there in front of Nina for me to quit being jealous. A lot of times she said it in front of Thad. It gave him the big head. While we waited for the bill, Momma went to the Ladies. That was the first time I had been with Nina without Momma.

"It's so sweet of you folks to want me along," Nina said. "I feel like part of the family."

"We feel the same," Lloyd said. He is always polite.

"I'm dying to meet Thad," Nina said, in that kittenish way of hers, lowering her lashes and ducking her head. "Clara says it'll be dangerous, though, because every woman falls in love with him."

"Momma has a tendency to exaggerate," I said.

Nina turned to me. "I envy you having Clara for a mother."

That gave me the opening. "You don't have a mother of your own?" I asked. "I guess we don't really know too much about you, do we, Lloyd?"

Lloyd smiled at Nina. "Enough."

Et tu, Brute, I wanted to say to him. I said, "Did you say you don't have a mother?"

"She died five years ago." I waited but Nina didn't go on.

"That's sad," I said, "what with you and your husband splitting up."

She gave me a funny look. "You want to know about my husband, don't you?" Her voice was not kittenish, but more like a growl. "He wasn't faithful, I couldn't stand it, and I left." She jutted her chin at me, daring me to ask more.

Lloyd said, "Lookee here: here comes Mrs. Blaine." He is a big heavy man, and when he jumped up so quick I thought the table was going with him.

On the ride back home to Montgomery, I said, "I know there's something unsavory that she doesn't want us to know about."

Lloyd said, "You ought to thank your lucky stars your momma has somebody she likes."

"Likes?" I said. "How about loves? How about worships?"

"Well, how about them?" he answered. "My goodness,

Jean, you got me, and that poor Nina hasn't got anybody."

There was no point arguing.

Momma called me the next morning before I went to church.

"I don't know what you said yesterday to Nina, but you sure did hurt her feelings. She spent half the evening telling me she might have to leave. What on earth did you say to her?"

"I asked about her kinfolks. Is that so bad? And I want to tell you she doesn't seem to have much in that line."

"Well, she has her brother's picture on her dresser. A nice looking red-headed man she says everybody calls Pinky. I bet you don't have your brother's picture on your dresser, speaking of kinfolks. Don't you dare tell Dinah this, but I sometimes wish Thad was single—he and Nina would just be wonderful together. You know how much fun Thad is. I can just see the three of us...."

"Is that what you called to tell me?" I said.

"No. I called to tell you to leave Nina alone. You had the poor thing upset all evening. You know how you are."

No sane person would blame me for hanging up then, and I didn't call back. Neither did she. We didn't speak for nearly two weeks. That's the longest we ever went except for eleven years ago when Thad and Dinah left their children with Momma while they went off to dig in some old ruins in Arizona. All they came back with was a handful of arrowheads. When I pointed out that I could have given them half a dozen arrowheads from my own back yard and so they had wasted Momma's time as well as their own, Momma told me to go home. That time we didn't speak for twenty-three days, and then I called and said I was sorry.

This time she called me. "This is too silly, Jean. I want to apologize for hurting your feelings. Nina says I only have one daughter and I better be nice to her."

"Tell Nina I am eternally grateful," I said, but she didn't get it.

She said, "Now's your turn to apologize for hurting mine."

"What did I do to hurt your feelings?"

"Love me, love my dog," she said.

"I can't love your..." I almost said bitch but I changed it in time and said, "...friend. I guess Lloyd and I better not be coming up there if we disturb Nina so bad."

"If you can't be nice, maybe you better not. But I've done my duty."

When it came time for our next visit and Momma didn't even mention it, I decided we wouldn't go. Lloyd said, "You're going to regret it if something happens to your momma."

I said, "Something already has: she has lost her mind over that Nina woman. She is in love."

We were out in the breeze-through, and Lloyd was sitting in the swing, reading the newspaper. That's his favorite place. Every once in a while he will look over the top of the paper at his roses. He said, "You're making a big mistake, honey. You can't win a battle if you don't have your troops on the battlefield."

I stood up so fast, I had to reach back to steady the rocker so it wouldn't fall. I said, "If you think I would lower myself to fight that Nina woman, you have another thought coming. And what business is it of yours, anyway?" I despise it when he takes Momma's part.

"It's my business all right," he said, crumbling the paper in his lap. Lloyd is very good-natured, but when you get him going, he is like a runaway freight train. "Who is it lives with you? Who is it sees that mouth of yours purse up? Who is it listens to you grinding down your molars at night? It's worse than when Thad is around."

"Thad is her son," I said to quiet him. "That is different."

Later I said, "All right, I'll join the battle, but I'm going to choose the battlefield. Instead of us going up there next month, we'll see if she'll come down here. Alone."

"That's the ticket. The two of you can have a good heart-to-heart for a few days."

∾

Lloyd had ordered a load of staples from a Birmingham con-
cern, and he figured he could fit it in the trunk of the car and
save the trucking cost and pick Momma up at the same time.
When I told Momma, she didn't seem all that eager. She said
she and Nina had tickets for a play series and she wasn't exactly sure when the next play was coming up, and they had
plans to get some fall clothes at one of those discount malls in
North Alabama, and the Crawfords were so crazy about Nina
that they wanted to have a party for her and of course
Momma had to be there and she didn't know when it was to
be.

And then she said, "Being as how little I like to be alone,
don't you think it would be selfish to leave Nina alone?"

I almost choked on that. "As you wish," I said. "Goodbye."

Momma called back the next day. "Nina says she won't
mind being alone a day or two. I can stay until Tuesday morning. Nina and I want to go to the picture show Tuesday night.
Promise you or Lloyd will bring me back on time."

I had quite a weekend laid out for us. We were going to a play
at the college the first night, I had planned a canasta party for
Saturday afternoon, and Saturday night we would go to a
movie. Sunday was church and then an air show at Maxwell
Field. And Monday we were going to do some discount shopping South Alabama style.

As soon as I saw Momma and Lloyd drive up, I ran out to
give her a big hug to show there were no hard feelings. Then
I escorted her to the room off the den that would have been
hers if she had lived with us. It was not a dinky back room. I
had fixed it all up with blues and pinks and new light-gray
wall-to-wall. I was sure she'd be pleased.

First thing she said was, "I'd like to use your telephone if
you don't mind." She went out to the kitchen.

I said to Lloyd, "She hasn't been in my house two minutes
before she has to call that Nina."

"Come on, Jeanie," Lloyd said. "Maybe she left a burner on."

"Phone's busy," Momma said when she came back.

"I fixed up your room in your favorite colors," I said.

"Thank you." She opened her overnight and shook out the blue silk dress she was going to wear to the play. "She never talks on the phone," she said.

"Probably when you're not around," I said.

"I guess I know her better than you do," Momma said sharply.

Just before we went out, Momma called again, but this time there wasn't any answer. Momma didn't say anything but she frowned and shook her head.

We had dinner at a nice steak house and went to see the students perform *Carousel*, one of my favorites. At the very first intermission, Momma said, "I'm real tired from the drive down. I've enjoyed the play, but can we go home now?"

Of course we could and we did. The minute we got in the house, she called Nina. But still no answer. She said, "Nina ought to be home. She wasn't going anywhere."

"Maybe she changed her mind," Lloyd said.

"Maybe," Momma said. "Or maybe she just won't answer. The truth is she's afraid of the telephone. Says it never brought her anything but bad news."

"Like what?" I asked.

"You'd like to know, wouldn't you?" Momma said.

"Beddybyes," Lloyd said, grabbing my elbow. "Nightnights."

The next morning I served my homemade buttermilk pancakes with blueberries. Momma had hardly gobbled hers down before she rushed off to the telephone. I heard her say, "Oh, I'm so sorry. I must have the wrong number."

When she came back to the breakfast nook, she said, "I'm going home."

"That's not fair," I said, and before I knew it I was

slumped over and crying.

Lloyd put his arm across my shoulder. "You're not giving Jean a chance, Mrs. Blaine."

Momma flapped her hand. "That's all foolishness, Lloyd. This has nothing to do with Jean. I'm worried about that girl. I told you she said the phone just brought bad news? Well, that husband of hers has been calling her. I thought I recognized his voice just then. He must be in my house."

"Maybe she wants him there," Lloyd said.

"Oh, no. She says he's a faithless flirt. Now, Lloyd, I guess it's only right for me to take the bus home since I'm a few days early."

But Lloyd said a promise was a promise, whether it was Saturday or Tuesday. He said just give him time to take the staples to the plant and keep a lunch date and by three o'clock he'd be ready.

"So we get there by nightfall," she said. "I won't worry until then."

I thought the whole thing was just like her: ruin our weekend and then expect Lloyd to drop everything to take her home.

It took the best part of an hour to call my friends to cancel the canasta party. I told them Momma was coming down with something—I sure would not tell them she was going home when she hadn't been in my house twenty-four hours. She and I didn't speak the rest of the morning. I made the tomato sandwiches and gave her hers and some ice tea without a word. I figured this was the end for us, mother or no. By the time Lloyd came home, I was so mad I had stopped being sad.

Lloyd took me aside and said, "Why don't you come with me?"

"Never ever," I said.

"We can come back by Montevallo and have a little visit with Sara. That ought to cheer you up."

"You know just how to get to me, Lloyd, for I do love my daughter," I said loud enough for Momma to hear.

We got to Momma's a little after dusk. Every light in the house was on. Momma went in first, with us following close behind. "Nina," she called. "Nina, honey, you here?" There wasn't a soul to be seen or heard.

We followed Momma into the kitchen. She pointed at the drainboard. "My best dishes," she said, "my best silver, my best crystal. I cannot believe my eyes."

"Did she break something?" Lloyd asked.

"That is not the point, Lloyd," she said. I had never heard her use that tone of voice with him before, though I had heard it for my benefit often enough. "She did not tell me she was planning to entertain while I was away. And everything is for two." For a minute she just stood there. Then she said, "I'm almost afraid to go upstairs."

And so Lloyd led the way. Nina's door was open, and we looked inside. The bed was a mess, the top sheet twisted around at the foot and pillows on the floor. A man's sock peeped out from under the bed. That reminded me of how Thad always left his socks and shoes anywhere he took them off. I remembered what Momma had said about Thad and Nina.

"She must have slept with him in that bed," Momma said. Her eyes drew in and flamed.

"Who? Thad?" I asked.

"Don't be a fool, Jean. I'm talking about that man. I cannot believe she would do such a hussy thing."

"They're still married, aren't they?" Lloyd asked.

Momma was too fired up to listen. "She will certainly have some tall explaining to do," she said. "I am very tolerant, but I will be a while forgiving this."

We began to look around. The closet was empty and there was not a cosmetic left except what had spilled on the dressing table Momma had moved in from my room. Then we noticed a piece of paper Scotch-taped to the mirror. Lloyd ripped it off and handed it to Momma. The two of us crowded around to read it over her shoulder:

Dear Clara,
I've gone back to Pinky (not my brother, sorry I lied). He's promised he won't fool around ever again. It was sure fun being with you. A port in a storm. I know you'll find someone else. Thanks for everything.
　　Nina

P.S. Forgive the mess. The plane to Memphis wouldn't wait!!!

Good riddance of bad rubbish, I thought. But I held my tongue. Let Momma speak first. I turned to her. Her eyes were stark open, as though they hadn't batted in a long time. "She's left me," she said, her face kind of collapsing. "She preferred him." She sat down at the dressing table and pressed her forehead down on the powder smudges on the glass top.

I couldn't help it. My heart went out and I leaned over and put my arms around her. She felt so tiny and limp I thought her bones had dissolved. She put her hand up and pressed mine.

She had her cry out in a minute or two, and then she sighed and straightened up. "I'm too upset to talk about it, so I'll just go to bed. See to things, please, Jean."

Lloyd and I cleaned up the bedroom, even turned over the mattress, and washed and put away all Momma's good things. Afterward, I fixed Lloyd and me scrambled eggs doctored with some yellow cheese. Then we went to bed in my old room, pulling out the trundle bed for Lloyd.

Lloyd said, "It's a good thing we never got hold of Sara. It sure would have disappointed her if she had of expected us to show and we didn't."

"Oh, she wouldn't have cared a bit. She has her friends," I answered. "I knew from the beginning that Nina was trouble. I could gloat if I wanted to, but I haven't said a word, have I?"

Lloyd just grunted. I was still full of talk, but once Lloyd sets his mind to sleep, you might as well shout at a bale of hay.

Sunday was hot early, and the three of us took our second cup of coffee to the front porch. I sat on the glider next to Momma and Lloyd sat in the wicker rocker.

Momma said, "I called Thad early this morning and told him what had happened."

Quick as a wink I said, "And is he on his way here to help you out?" I knew he wasn't, never had been, never would be.

She said, "Dinah wanted me to come visit. She was so sweet."

"I wonder how long that'd last, with you cuddling up to Thad every minute."

"Oh, I'm not going," Momma said. "You don't have to fret about that."

I said, "I believe I've still got the telephone number of that Oneonta woman."

"I don't want any Oneonta woman," Momma said. "It hurt me too bad for Nina to treat me that way. I'm getting old, Jean, too old to let my feelings get all riled up."

I felt my heart begin to pound. "Momma," I said, "what exactly do you mean?"

"I'm moving to Montgomery with you. I've been thinking about it all night. You're the one person I can count on."

"Oh, Momma, I'm so glad." I felt the tears welling up behind my eyes. I put my arm around her and drew her to me.

I won't pretend a thought or two about Thad didn't pass through my mind. I imagined myself inviting him to pay us a short visit. I saw him and Lloyd standing out near Lloyd's roses, Lloyd so big, Thad so puny. And I saw myself politely passing him a glass of ice tea with a slice of lemon hanging on the lip. And he would know that I had graciously let him come to my house to see my mother. I could no more have got the grin off my face than I could have run without toes.

I said, "We're going to have us some fun, I can tell you. Don't for a minute think Birmingham's got it all—Montgomery is a pret-ty lively place. I can just see the two of us going to plays and playing cards and buying discount clothes."

I heard a little moan, and I looked over at Lloyd. His face was red and swollen as though his allergies were acting up.

"What's the matter?" I asked.

"What about me?" he said, in a choked voice. "What about me? What about me?"

"Why, Lloyd," Momma said in that sweet way of hers, "you're just as jealous as you can be." And we sat there, Momma and me, holding and gliding, gliding and holding, and smiling at him.

I Never Said a Word

AFTER Momma had been with us about a year, she decided she might have a heart attack if she didn't go see Thad in Oklahoma where he was stationed. She said she wouldn't fly, not because she was afraid but because she didn't want to look down through all that air. And she sure didn't want to travel on the train that far by herself.

"You know I won't talk to strangers plotting no-telling-what devilment. Haven't I all your life told you never?" she said. "You'd think just this one time you'd oblige me, Jean."

I did not want to accompany her. Watching her bill and coo over Thad is one of my least favorite occupations. Momma thinks Thad could have discovered Coca-Cola if it hadn't already been discovered or been Pope if we were Roman instead of Baptist. She has always been partial to him over me. Poppa's sister Nettie once said the only reason Momma gave me the titty when I was a baby was so Thad could get his sleep and be real smart for first grade next day. Yet who was it she lived with? You can bet the last drop in the bucket it wasn't Thad and Dinah.

I said, "Who'd cook for Lloyd?"

"If he didn't eat a single bite while we were gone he would still need to diet," she answered. "Surely to mercy he is not so selfish he can't do without you one week in twenty-seven years."

I said, "Lloyd is not selfish at all."

"Did I say he was? You are as touchy as a boil."

Just then I heard Lloyd's Oldsmobile crunching on the driveway. It was a hot day, and Momma and I were sitting in our breeze-through, sipping ice tea with lemon and mint from my own garden. For the time Momma had been with us, we hadn't turned on the air conditioning because it dried her throat. She said anyway the breeze-through never failed to provide a breeze, even when it was so hot cornstalks fell flat to the ground.

I got up to fix Lloyd his ice tea. When I got back out, he was twirling his Panama hat and staring at the brim. I knew she had broached the subject.

"My grandchildren will be grown and off to college before I see them again, if I ever do," Momma said. "And Thad may get moved to another post and not have the general's house." Thad was a colonel, but he was head of the post and had the main house. When Lloyd had said it must not be much of a post if a colonel could run it, Momma did not speak to him for three days.

I handed Lloyd his glass, and he set it down on the bare top of the wicker table instead of the straw coaster I had put there for the express purpose of soaking up the moisture. I reached over and set the glass on the coaster.

"But a whole week?" Lloyd said. "Company's like fish—it goes bad after three days." He grinned as if he had made that up himself.

"I'm not going halfway across America for three days, fish or no fish," Momma answered, flipping her chin at him. "But never mind. I don't have to go."

She got up and flounced into the house.

Once you let Momma's pouts get up a head of steam, no matter what you do she won't quit until your feelings are black and blue all over. I figured I would only have to watch her worshiping Thad for a week, but she might pout for a month.

I said, "Hurry, now, Lloyd, before she gets going."

"Okay, Mrs. Blaine," he shouted, "Jean'll go with you."

He took a big swig of ice tea, the glass sweat dribbling down his front and puckering his shirt. Then, staring right at me, he carefully placed the glass back on the bare table.

You would have thought the sleeping car porter and the dining car waiter and even the two strange men who shared our table had nothing better to do than listen to Momma talk about Thad. Thad at West Point, Thad getting a medal in Vietnam, Thad living in the general's house. She even said nice things about Dinah, how smart she dressed and how she played golf real well. And then on and on about Bitsy and Temple like they were well-mannered geniuses, not the hellions I remembered from three years before. Of course Momma never told how Dinah's family dominated the names. Bitsy's real name was Dinah, and Temple was Dinah's maiden name.

Back in our compartment, I said, "It hurts my feelings you never mention Sara and Carl and Lloyd."

She said, "Sakes, Jean, *you* could mention your family if you wanted them mentioned so bad. There's nobody but me to defend Thad and his. I hope you are not going to be so dag touchy once we get there."

"I just won't say a word," I said.

Thad was waiting on the platform as the train chugged in. He had on blue shorts and a short-sleeve plaid shirt and barefoot sandals. "You'd have thought he would have worn his uniform," Momma said. "Those men will think I was fibbing. But don't let's say a word about it."

Thad was always slight, from Momma's side, but the baggy shorts looked so big on him I thought he could have whirled around inside without touching the cloth. He sure didn't look military.

"He looks might puny to be an officer in the army," I said.

"Slim. Not fat like some," Momma retorted.

The porter came in to see to our suitcases. He was a tall colored man with one droopy eyelid that gave him a sad look. Momma reached for her purse. "It's only fair I should be the one to tip the sleeping car porter, seeing as you tipped the dining car and anyway it's my son we came to visit." She stuck two one-dollar bills in the ashtray. I let her get off first, and then I added two tens to the two ones.

When I got out on the platform, Momma was still holding on to Thad, looking at him as though he was Clark Gable— Thad is only average in looks.

When Thad pulled loose so we could peck each other's cheek, Momma said, "Where are Dinah and the children? Surely the children wanted to come welcome their Granny."

Thad looked around as though he might have just lost track of them, and then he laughed a little and said, "The car isn't really big enough for everybody."

The porter loaded our suitcases on a shopping cart Thad had found, and Momma said, "Jean, count the grips."

I was embarrassed, with the man standing right there, but I counted them out loud to satisfy her. Thad opened his wallet and gave the porter a twenty-dollar bill, as though he thought we didn't have sense enough to know to tip. I decided to let him just waste his money.

All the way from the station, Momma sat in front with her hand on Thad's shoulder, as though she was afraid he was going to run away. We drove down some tree-lined streets and went through a gate. When a soldier saluted, Momma squealed and smacked Thad's thigh. "I'm as proud as a sow with a prize shoat," she said.

Thad stopped the car in front of a little red brick bungalow with white trim and three dormer windows poking out of the roof. "Is this the head general's house?" Momma asked. "It's so puny."

Thad said, "It's what the army provides, Momma."

Momma said in her quick little voice, "Are those shorts

and sandals what the army provides, too?"

Thad laughed. "Don't you think I have pretty legs?"

"Not pretty enough to be parading through town so everybody including your own soldiers can see you."

Thad just grinned at her.

By the time we made it up the walk, Dinah had come out to greet us. "You look so cool and pretty in that pink dress," Momma called. "Just lovely." She looked at Thad to see how he took the compliment, but he was busy with the luggage.

After Dinah had hugged and kissed us, she drew us inside the house. The house was nice enough, but not nearly so pretty as what Momma was accustomed to. I could see she was disappointed.

After we had finished complimenting the house and the furniture, Dinah said, "Wouldn't you like to rest?"

"I can rest at home where there isn't much else to do," Momma answered.

I did not want Thad and Dinah to think Montgomery was still just a sleepy old town, and so I said, "There is plenty to do in Montgomery."

"But we've already done it," Momma said.

Just then the front door swooshed open and in walked a tallish, skinny boy about fourteen. His hair was as green as a grasshopper and stood up in spikes all over this head. Momma put her hand to her throat.

"Temple," she murmured. "Is *that* Temple?"

"The one, the only, the original," said Temple, with a bow.

When he went over to hug Momma, she gave his hair a pat and then jerked her hand away as though she had spotted a water bug crawling on his scalp. "Is that your hair's natural color?" she asked in a disgusted voice.

Dinah said, "The kids do their hair that way now."

Momma stared at her. "And what do you think of it, Thad?"

Thad laughed. "I wouldn't do it to mine, but it's his hair."

"But he is your son," Momma said. "The son of the commander-in-chief of the whole post."

Dinah looked at Thad and Thad looked at Dinah. Dinah said, "I bet you'd like to change your shoes. If it weren't for feet, traveling would be fun."

"I'll take your luggage upstairs," Temple said. "They're going to be in Bitsy's room, aren't they, Pop?"

"But what about Bitsy?" I asked.

"Her room is the only one with two beds, and anyway she really prefers to sleep in the study," Thad said. "Then she can stay up all night watching cable television."

Momma said, "I hear there are awful things on some of the cables."

Nobody said a word.

Momma took off her shoes and lay down on the bed. "That is one funny-looking boy," she said. "I wonder if people in town know he's Thad's son."

"Maybe they think he's just Dinah's."

"Now, Jean," she began, but she was already half asleep.

I didn't feel comfortable in that house, but I figured the best way to get over feeling ill at ease was to pretend not to be. So I went back downstairs. Dinah and Thad were sitting on the side porch, reading the newspaper.

"Well, Jean," Thad said, putting down the paper, "I appreciate all you and Lloyd are doing for Momma." I didn't say anything. I wasn't doing it for him, so there was no call to say he was welcome.

"Is it working out?" Dinah asked.

"Just wonderful," I answered. "Sometimes I think Lloyd believes Momma is his momma. He's taking the both of us to Pompano Beach when we get back. He says he's going to make her buy a bikini."

Thad said, "Wouldn't you and Lloyd like to take a vacation by yourselves?"

"We don't need a vacation by ourselves."

Thad smiled. "Maybe Momma does. Dinah and I were

thinking she might like to stay on with us a while."

Thad had never mentioned one word about keeping Momma. But he had always been sly. "I don't know if she'd change her plans," I said. "She is pretty set in her ways."

"We'll give her two or three days before we say anything about it, then. Let her feel comfortable and get to know the place a little."

"And maybe you better get to know her. She can be mighty touchy."

"Really?" Thad said. "I never had any problems with her. She's feisty, but she always seems so cheerful."

I said, "She can get very pouty with family." His smile said he didn't believe a word of it.

"I hope the trip out was pleasant," Dinah said. "We were so pleased when she told us you wanted to come with her. You don't play golf, do you?"

"When would I ever find time?" I asked. "Looking after Momma is a full-time job."

Bitsy didn't get home until we were sitting down to dinner. She was a year older than Temple and almost as bad looking. Her blondish hair hung limp halfway down her back and was coated with something oily. She had colored her skin greasy gray and even had on greasy gray lipstick. She was a little bit of a thing, not a hundred pounds nor five feet tall.

Momma hugged her and then said, "Don't they feed you enough, honey? You come visit me—I'll put some flesh on those bones." Bitsy looked a dagger at her mother.

During dinner, Momma talked to Thad steady, breaking off every once in a while to tell Bitsy and Temple something heroic or hilarious their father had done when he was a boy. Bitsy sighed and rolled her eyes, but Temple laughed at everything. He had a funny laugh, a cross between a yelp and a chicken's cackle.

When we finished the lemon pie, I stood up to clear the table. Dinah said, "Stay seated, you're guests."

Momma shook her head. "Oh, no. We're family. We'll do our part, won't we, Jean?" She nodded for me to go on clearing.

Dinah said, "Bitsy will help." Bitsy shot another dagger, but she went around to get Momma's plate.

Momma took hold of Bitsy's forearm. "Jean can help. I want me and Bitsy to get acquainted again. You sit right down and tell me all about yourself." Bitsy just stood holding the plate until I went over and shoved a chair under her. Momma said, "What do you like best in all the world? Is it still riding in the dodgem cars at the fair?"

Temple cackled and said, "No. It's stand with her friends on the corner of First Avenue and Lincoln to watch the soldiers go by." He caught the dagger this time.

Momma laughed. "And I guess you like to stand kitty-corner and watch the girls watch the soldiers."

Temple waved his arms in the air and rolled his eyes up. "I wouldn't watch those dogs," he said.

"Now, Temple," Thad said, smiling, wagging his finger.

"I was talking about girls," Momma said. "What you liked second best was playing cards. Anybody for a hot game of hearts tonight?" She made as though she was shuffling and dealing a pack of cards.

Temple said, "I got a big date, Granny."

Bitsy said, "I have to meet somebody about something." The two of them flew out of the house as though they had just been let out of jail.

"You let those children go out at night by themselves?" Momma asked. Thad just laughed.

Momma and Thad went out on the screened-in side porch and Dinah and I went into the kitchen. I had never spent much time with Dinah. She was born in Detroit and lived five years in New York City, and that has got to make a difference. Usually when I talk with other ladies, I tell them what Sara and Carl are up to, but I thought Dinah might think I was trying to make her feel bad. We tried a few conversations that didn't work very well, and we were both glad to join the others.

"The younguns out here seem to lead busy lives," Momma said. "I was kind of surprised they didn't want to stay home."

"They're almost grown, you know. They come and go pretty much as they wish."

Momma said, "You're still paying the bills, aren't you?"

"Now, Momma," Thad began, but then he just smiled.

"We want them to be with us when they want to be with us," said Dinah. "Then we all enjoy quality time."

The next day we didn't see Temple and Bitsy at all. We left before they were up, and they were gone when we got back. It was a Saturday, and Thad and Dinah took us for a trip to a state park in the hills. When Thad turned on the car air conditioner, I said,

"Air conditioning dries out Momma's throat, Thad."

Momma turned from the front seat to where I was sitting in back with Dinah and looked at me so hard you would have thought I had taken the Lord's name in vain. "Don't be silly," she said. She gave Thad's knee a little pat. "Of course you need air conditioning. At home even when it's hot, it's so green and pretty you don't feel it. Out here's hot and dry enough to turn your skin to crocodile." Two thoughts must have hit head-on: Nina and the fact that she wasn't being very tactful. "Of course pretty skin is only skin-deep." Then she turned around to us again. "You sure keep your skin nice, Dinah."

Dinah laughed. "I hope you don't think my nice is only skin deep." It took Momma about five minutes to explain she didn't mean that *at all*.

We ate at the park cafe, and then we drove around some more and went home. Momma and Thad did the talking, Momma mostly, though Thad always answered her questions—I'll give him that. Dinah and I just looked at the scenery, poor as it was.

Pretty much the same thing happened Sunday, only we went in the opposite direction, not even as nice because it wasn't a state park. We stopped for lunch in a cafe in a little dusty town. Momma ordered a fried egg sandwich because she said there wasn't anything bad they could do to an egg except cook it rotten and she would detect that before she swallowed. Thad ordered a steak sandwich and Dinah ordered tuna fish. I thought it was only polite to show I wasn't afraid of the food, so I ordered tuna fish also. It was perfectly all right.

On the way home, Momma said, "I like sightseeing, but I'd like to see my grandchildren, too, funny hair and all. They're not avoiding me, are they?"

Dinah looked horrified. "Of course not. Thad has to be at his office tomorrow so the rest of us'll stay home and you'll see more than enough of them."

Momma woke me up early the next morning—she said she thought she heard reveille and everybody would be up. We went downstairs and made ourselves some coffee and toast, and then Momma sat at the kitchen table and wrote about twenty postcards she had bought at the park.

When Thad walked in about eight-thirty, Momma frowned and batted her hand at him. "Shoo, Thad, I got up early so I could see you in your real uniform."

He had on a light green shirt and dark green pants. He could have passed for a farm hand, except his shoes were shined and he had his colonel's pins on his shoulders.

"This is what we wear in the summer." He pecked Momma's cheek and was gone.

"Seems you missed your beauty sleep for nothing," I said. For once she didn't have a quick reply.

We spent the morning on the porch, Momma doing crochet and me reading a mystery. Dinah excused herself to go to the grocery store. When she got home, we sat down to some cold cut meats and cheeses and lettuce and tomatoes. Just as we

36

were fixing our sandwiches, Temple came down. His spiky hair was bent every which of a way, and he still had sleep in his eyes.

Momma said, "You don't wash your face and comb your hair before you appear in public?"

He grinned and said, "I didn't know this was public. I thought it was my home sweet home."

"When you have guests, that is public," Momma said. She looked as though she had him there.

Dinah laughed. "But you said you're family."

Momma looked around the room. "Anything I say will be held against me. I was just trying to teach him some manners. But I guess that's not any of my business."

Dinah colored to the roots of her hair. "Of course it's your business," she said. "You're his Granny."

"I have plenty of manners," Temple said, "but I don't want to use them up on family when I might really need them sometime."

"Manners are like muscles," Momma said, shooting Temple a little triumphant look. "Exercise makes them stronger."

Temple cackled. "Hey, you're not so dumb after all." He reached over and patted the top of her head. Momma drew away from him and pressed her lips together.

Just then Bitsy came in, and if Temple was still half in bed, Bitsy was three-quarters out the door. She had that gray stuff on her face and lips, and hot as it was she was wearing a long, frayed, greenish cloak grabbed at the neck with one of those things they call frogs and the hood hanging down her back.

"Where on earth did you get such a garment as that?" Momma asked. I could tell she was trying to make her voice just interested, not judgmental.

"Goodwill," Bitsy muttered. She poured herself some orange juice from a carton in the refrigerator and drank it standing up.

Momma looked disbelieving. "You don't mean you wear other folks' rags?"

"Goodwill is Bitsy's favorite boutique," Temple said.

Dinah said, "It's sort of a costume."

"Granny likes it so well you should give it to her," Temple said.

"I would not let it touch my body." Momma stepped back as though to be sure it didn't touch even her hand. Bitsy closed her eyes, and I thought she was falling back asleep.

I said, "Bitsy, would you like me to fix you a salami sandwich?"

Her eyes popped open. "For *breakfast?*" she asked. She put her hand over her mouth and gagged. I forbore to tell her it was lunchtime.

"Fix me one," said Temple. "Mustard pickles mayo tomatoes salt and pepper rye bread relish some of that cheese lots of lettuce no sprouts hold the onions."

"I be glad to," I said, laughing. "But you'll have to say again what you want on it."

"I heard him," Momma said. "I'll fix it." She grabbed the cold cut plate right out of my hand.

Temple cackled. "Fight over me. Pull each other's hair. Spit at each other. Draw blood."

"Oh, be quiet," said Bitsy. She turned to Momma. "Don't you find Temple just a little...bizarre?"

Temple flapped in his chair and screeched, "Don't answer that."

"I wouldn't for the world," Momma said.

And then Temple and Bitsy began to laugh, and they went on until they were crying. I had to grin with them. It was the first time I had seen Bitsy anything but ready to bite nails in half.

Dinah smiled, too. When she saw the expression on Momma's face, she said, "What they're laughing at is, not answering was really answering yes, you do think...."

"I know what they are laughing at," Momma said. She did

not smile back at Dinah.

"If you don't think Temple is bizarre, Granny," said Bitsy, "then you must be bizarre yourself."

"I don't doubt you think that," said Momma. During the commotion she had gone on fixing the sandwich and now she shoved it toward Temple.

"Being bizarre is Temple's secret ambition," said Bitsy, "not that he has to try very hard."

"Don't break my heart by saying I'm normal," Temple said to Momma. He dropped his face onto his sandwich and began to sob.

Momma turned to Dinah. "Is this what you meant by quality time?" She got up and went out on the porch. We all watched as she sat down, opened her tote bag, and drew out her crocheting.

After a minute, Dinah said, "Maybe you two ought to go out there and apologize."

Bitsy said, "What did I do to apologize for?"

Dinah said, "She might appreciate it if you showed her a little attention."

"But that's what we were doing," Temple said.

Dinah turned to me. "You know her ways so much better than I do. What should we do? How should we handle this?"

I just shrugged. If Thad never had any problems with Momma, far be it from me to say a word.

Momma spent most of the afternoon crocheting in our room. By the time Thad got home, she was in a good pout. When she pouts, her face gets stiff and her lips vanish inside her mouth. She gives one-word answers to questions and will not look anybody in the eye.

At dinner, everybody tried to pretend nothing was wrong. Thad kept asking Momma did she remember this and that, but Momma had lost her memory. Even Bitsy did her share of the talking, volunteered to clear the table, and did not leave the house for a half an hour after we finished eating.

39

And Temple was truly bizarre. After dinner he went up-stairs and turned some of that green hair into purple and shaved off a strip down the middle so it looked like someone had mowed through tall grass. We all laughed—except Momma. She glanced at Temple and then right back down to her crocheting.

Thad slapped his hands on the top of his thighs and said, "One thing this town has is the best damn ice cream in the world. Let's go get some."

Dinah jumped up as though that was the most brilliant idea anybody had ever had. Momma said, "Let the others go. The car isn't big enough for everybody. That's why they couldn't come to the station." That was the longest speech of the day for her. Thad and Dinah looked at each other, and Thad motioned Dinah to sit back down.

"I meant just you and me, Momma."

Momma said, "I'm not hungry, thank you."

The whole room just sagged.

When we were lying in bed, Momma said, "I never knew such bad-behaved children in my life. They ignored me for two days, and then they laughed at me. And the way they look. What would you have done if Carl painted his hair that way?"

"Carl has better sense than that," I said. "And Lloyd and I would not have let him in the first place." There was no point in mentioning Carl's pierced ear—the hole was almost closed.

"Bitsy looks like a vampire had sucked her blood. And so ill-natured. I don't remember Sara ever going through a stage like that."

"We wouldn't have allowed that either," I said, though Sara is not easy to allow or not allow.

"Those younguns are all Temple," Momma said. "I'm glad they didn't think to name that boy Butterfield." Butterfield is Momma's maiden name. "People from Detroit just don't think the way we do."

"I don't think you can put all the blame on Detroit," I

said. "They're Thad's children, too. And you'd think with Thad being an army officer...."

"He may be commander-in-chief of the post," Momma said, "but he is not the commander-in-chief of his own home." She was silent for a while, and then she said, "Unless you mind, we'll go home tomorrow."

I said I didn't mind.

We went downstairs early the next morning, and I called the railroad company. Sure enough they could route us all the way through to Montgomery. So I called Lloyd—collect of course—to tell him we would be there the next day.

Lloyd laughed and said, "But I still have some ham left." Lloyd hates ham, but what else can you leave somebody for a week who won't turn on a burner for himself?

When Thad came in, Momma said, "Jean called home and Lloyd is sick, so we're going home today. We'll be leaving in about an hour and a half if you will kindly take us to the station."

Thad looked as though a flea was biting him in a private place he could not scratch. "I know the children are boisterous," he said, "but they didn't mean any harm. Dinah said they just got carried away."

"Oh, I forgot that the minute it happened," Momma said. "It's just Lloyd is sick. And you know I dearly love Lloyd—he has been an angel to me. I could not stay here and let him be sick alone."

Thad argued with her some, pointing out he hadn't taken her to the Officer's Club yet and he wanted her to meet the town mayor and he thought she might enjoy going to the rifle range with him. Momma said she was too old for the Officer's Club, she had once met the mayor of Birmingham, which was a bigger city, and she didn't like the sound of guns going off like in a battle.

As a final effort, Thad said, "But Lloyd will probably be well by the time you get there."

"Not if we hurry," Momma said.

Thad shifted from one leg to the other and sighed, and then he went back up the steps. Momma gave me one of her little triumphant grins, and I was almost sorry for Thad. I could hear him rummaging around upstairs, waking this one and that one. Dinah came running down the stairs in her bathrobe.

"You aren't leaving?" she said as though that was the most difficult thing in the world for anybody to manage. "We were hoping you'd stay for at least...." She didn't get to finish because Bitsy and Temple rushed in, still in pajamas.

Temple said, "Hey, Granny, don't go yet. I got some magenta hair dye and a lot of other bizarre things I want to try out for you."

Bitsy said, "And I was thinking that maybe this afternoon you'd go stand with me at First and Lincoln to watch the soldiers go by. Or else we could play hearts."

It was pretty lame, but I give them credit for making the effort. "Not this time," Momma said. But she gave them each a little pat.

Just then Thad walked in. He had on his uniform with his belt slanted from his shoulder to his waist and a row of ribbons and as much braid as I had ever seen. It was funny how that uniform made him look less puny. Momma went over to him and hugged him tight. She said, "Now you look like a real commander-in-chief." I have to admit that once Momma gets her victory, she sets her pout aside and is downright gracious. She can even sometimes change her mind.

I said, "Momma, we better get to our packing. If we miss the train, we'll have to fly."

"Get dressed," Thad directed Bitsy and Temple. "You'll go with me to put your grandmother on the train."

Momma looked from Bitsy to Temple and back, a worried look growing on her face. "We'll leave the way we came. We don't need a big send-off, do we, Jean?" I knew she didn't want people on the train to see her with Bitsy and Temple.

☙

Thad and Dinah took us to the station. Momma wouldn't sit in front, saying, "That's the wife's rightful place." When we got to the little station, we had to hurry because the train was already in. We were in luck: the sleeping car porter with the droopy eye was standing right outside our car. He ran over to help us, no doubt thinking he would get another forty-two dollars, which he did not.

Momma was deep in thought all day, and of course I didn't want to gloat. She crocheted and I read two mysteries. Dinah had fixed us some cold meat sandwiches and packed some fruit for us, so we didn't have to go to the dining car.

About eight o'clock, the sleeping car porter came to open our beds. Momma smiled at him and said, "I remember you from the trip out." She cocked her head and gave him a sympathetic smile. "Is your eye feeling better?"

"Yes'm," he said.

"That was my son in the uniform," Momma said. "Did I tell you about him being head of the post?"

"Yes'm," the porter said.

"He has so many medals from the Vietnamese War he can hardly hold his chest up."

"Yes'm," the porter said.

"There wasn't room in the car for his children. It was real sad because they just begged to see us to the station."

"Little children do love trains," the porter said. "You ladies step in the hall I'll fix your bed."

After we turned out the lights and lay in the dark a few minutes, Momma said, "If you hadn't been there, I believe none of it would have happened."

"Now, Momma," I said real quick. "I didn't do anything."

"Did I say you did? It's just sometimes having an odd person around changes things."

"So now I'm an odd person?"

43

"I am not talking about you as a person," she said. "You are so dag sensitive. What I meant was, I could tell Thad didn't like the children being so boisterous, but with an odd person around he didn't want to put his foot down."

I said, "Maybe he was afraid if he put his foot down, someone would stomp on it. Like you said, he doesn't run that establishment."

She rustled in bed. "Honestly, Jean, I cannot have a sensible conversation with you about your brother," she said.

I didn't want her to start up a pout, so I didn't say another word. I just lay there and listened to the train rattling toward home.

The Boy Friend

SARA decided that after she graduated from the University of Montevallo she would go straight to Atlanta to work for Brotherhood Life Insurance. Lloyd and I didn't want Momma to ruin Sara's graduation day, and so we didn't tell her about Atlanta until after the ceremony when we went back to the dormitory for Sara to finish packing. Momma and I were sitting on the bare mattress, fanning ourselves with our purses and ballooning our skirts a tad to cool our legs. Whoever invented nylons must not have tried them out on a humid June afternoon in Alabama or they would surely have destroyed the recipe.

Momma said, "You want me to drive home with you in your new Chevy car, Sara honey?" We had given the car to Sara for graduating.

Sara shot me an I-told-you-you-should-have-told-her look. I said, "Sara's not going home. She's got a job in Atlanta."

Momma shifted on her hip so I would see her face. She looked as though I had insulted her personally. "You are sending this innocent child to live in that city full of drugs and misfits?"

Lloyd said, "We're not sending her, Mrs. Blaine. She's going on her own."

To tell the truth, Lloyd and I didn't ourselves much like the idea—Sara being only twenty-two—but there wasn't much we could do short of hog-tying her. Dainty and pretty as she

45

is, she has a mind of her own. When she was a little bit of a thing, if she didn't get her way, she would hold her breath until she turned blue in the face and fainted. When she was nearly ten, Lloyd said she wouldn't ever willingly surrender a powerful weapon like that, so we might as well put up the white flag. The next time it happened he promised her a ten speed bicycle with a speedometer on condition she never hold her breath again. Except once or twice, when perhaps she was reminding us of the weapon, she kept her word.

"What's wrong with Montgomery or at least Birmingham?" Momma asked.

Sara threw the last of her undies into a cardboard carton. "Birmingham is a has-been steel mill," she said, "and Montgomery should have stayed capital of the Confederacy for all the places it's going."

When Momma can't think of anything to say, she says it to me. "Jean, aren't you ashamed to send that child off without any supervision?"

"Now you get the point," Sara said as she cinched the carton with a crackly leather belt. "Get with it, Granny. It's almost the twenty-first century."

Momma threw her hands heavenward. "I will thank my maker for calling me before the twenty-first comes if it keeps coming on like this."

"Now, y'all," I said, flapping my hand at them. Sara and Momma are more alike than either is like me. They are small and quick and as feisty as a terrier on a diet of beans. They dearly love each other, but Momma will express her opinion and Sara will express hers. I sometimes feel I am the no-man's land and they are the barb wire on both sides.

Just then a tall young man knocked on the open door and walked in. I knew at once it was Sara's beau, Bobby Jenkins. Over Sara's spring vacation he had telephoned two or three times, but we had never met him in the flesh. Not that there was much flesh to meet. He was skin and bones, with an Adam's apple so prominent that when he spoke you would have thought a little kitten was playing inside his throat.

We all shook hands with him and said we were pleased to meet him, and then nobody could think of anything to say, except Momma. When she meets new people, she's always able to muster up her social talents. She said, "Now, Bobby, tell the truth: what do you think of this sweet little thing going off to live alone in Atlanta?"

"You don't need to worry none," said Bobby, his Adam's apple shooting up and down. "I'mo be there to look after her."

Lloyd rested his elbows on the chiffonier and began to scrape his thumbnail over the tips of his fingernails to get the roughness off. I have given him a dozen nail files and a thousand emery boards, but if something is bothering him, he will go to scraping.

At near-dusk, Sara drove off in her new Chevy, and Bobby followed on his motorcycle. Sara had told us Bobby was going on into Atlanta to stay with a cousin and she was going to spend the night on the outskirts with her freshman year roommate. Monday she would start looking for an apartment.

As we watched the taillights disappear, Momma said, "It's none of my business."

"What isn't?" Lloyd asked in a mournful tone.

He opened the side door and settled Momma in the front passenger seat of our car. She says when she is up front like that, she can see quicker if there's going to be a wreck and jump out in time. She didn't answer Lloyd until he was behind the wheel and I was settled in back. Then she said, "It's none of my business that boy in Atlanta with her and no supervision, but I would have thought it was yours."

Lloyd sighed. "The child's an adult and's got to lead her own life, Mrs. Blaine."

"Suppose she wanted to be a harlot," Momma said real quick. "Would you just sit by for that, too?"

"Well, since she doesn't want to be a harlot," Lloyd said, putting the car in gear, "I don't have to answer that one."

47

That stopped Momma, and so she turned to me and said, "I know times change, but some things are still right and some things are still wrong. Surely you admit that, Jean."

I said I did.

"And surely you admit that twenty-two is a dangerous age."

I said I did.

We were out on the highway by then. Momma does not like air-conditioning, and to keep from smothering to death we all had to lower our windows so that hot air was blowing in our faces. There was so much air noise I almost felt alone. I got to thinking about how when I was twenty-two. I pictured me and Lloyd down there in Tampa at that motel, when I was supposed to be in Sarasota visiting I-couldn't-right-off-re-member-her-name, but she had been a good friend then and would have told Momma I was swimming or gone to the movies if Momma had called. She didn't.

There were other memories of danger from that time that I didn't much like to think about, and so I began to hum to myself. I could not remember what came after "Friendship, friendship, just a perfect blendship."

Up front Momma was going on and on about the young. She was shouting to make sure I heard. She said it was the parents' fault because they just didn't care any more. In her day, she said, people looked after their children until they got good and settled with their own family. She said she might have expected it of me because I had always given in to Sara, but she was surprised at Lloyd.

"Lloyd's easier on Sara than I am," I shouted.

"Then he'll pay the consequences," she said.

Lloyd said, "We trust Sara."

"It's not Sara," Momma said. "It's that gawky boy. Who is he anyway? Does he have any people?"

"Must," said Lloyd. "Everybody has people."

"I'm talking about decent people. But if you don't care, I won't say another word. Except this: if it was my Jean, I would call to make sure she got to where she was supposed to get to."

Lloyd laughed. "Where else would she get to?"

"To a tourist court," Momma shouted in a triumphant voice.

It was dark when we entered Montgomery's city limits. With motels lining both sides of the highway and neon flashing, it did not look much like the Confederate capital. We had been up since six and were tired, and when we got home Momma went straight to her room next to the den and we went upstairs to ours.

Lloyd sat on the bed and took off his shoes and socks. Then he said, "Do we have that roommate's number?"

"Lloyd!" I said. "You'll no such."

He shook his head vigorously. "I just want to check if she had car trouble."

"A brand new Chevy?" I said. "And if she did, Bobby was there to help."

When he glanced up at me, his face was as long and weary as a basset hound's.

About a month later, Sara decided to come home for a weekend, and to bring Bobby with her. Lloyd said she ought to come by herself the first time. I pointed out that since the purpose of the trip was to pick up her books and tapes, it was a good thing Bobby was coming to help her.

"My back's not broken," Lloyd said.

Momma and Lloyd and I talked about the visit for the whole week before. Sara had had several beaux, but they hadn't lasted long enough for her to bring one home before. The big question was where Bobby would sleep, downstairs on the pull-out in the den right next to Momma's room or upstairs in our son Carl's old room.

"You are not using the head God gave you," Momma said. "He would have to share the bathroom with Sara."

I laughed. "Maybe they could take turns instead of both being in there at once."

Lloyd scrunched his face. "Your momma's got a point,

Jean. Let's put him in the den."

"Then he would have to share the bathroom with Momma, and he might spy on her." I winked, but he didn't wink back.

"It would not be as much temptation," he said.

So I gave up that line and went to another. "If they were going to misbehave, wouldn't they already have done it in Atlanta?"

"You ought to be ashamed of yourself," Momma said. "The idea of accusing Sara of misbehaving."

"No," I said, "you were the one...." I stopped. Pinning Momma down to what she had said was like using one finger to catch an eel.

Sara and Bobby were to drive over after work that Friday, and about ten o'clock we heard the car tires crunch the gravel on the driveway. The three of us went to stand on the porch. "Look who's driving," Momma said. It was Bobby.

"Now, Momma," I said, but Lloyd had already looked.

"We didn't give that car to him," he muttered.

I thought I ought to stomp that weed before it got big, and so I said, "What if they had driven up on Bobby's motorcycle?"

That quieted Lloyd, but Momma said, "I wouldn't have been a bit surprised."

While Bobby got their suitcases out of the trunk, Sara ran up to give us our hello-kisses. I held on to her for quite a while. When a child comes home after a long spell away, it is the greatest pleasure in the world, even if it doesn't last but the first day.

As Bobby came up the walk, he shouted, "Which way to the den? Sara said you'd be putting me in the den so I can share the bathroom with Granny."

I had to laugh, but it miffed Lloyd. He said, "I believe you will find the den quite comfortable."

Sara turned to Momma. "But don't you dare use his towel,

Granny. He is real particular about that." She gave Bobby a kind of back-handed slap on his belly, and they both laughed real loud.

Lloyd said, "I'll take your suitcase up, Sara," but before he could grab it, Bobby had it.

"Can't I even *see* the upstairs?" he said, his Adam's apple racing up and down. "I promise I won't stay more than two minutes."

Sara whapped his belly again. "Now *that* is speed." They both laughed again. It is funny how your children think you don't have sense enough to understand their jokes even when they are said in plain English.

As the three of them climbed the steps, Momma frowned and said, "I can't believe she said that." I was startled that Momma had understood, too. She shook her head. "I have never in all my born days used anybody else's towel."

Momma was already sitting in the breakfast nook when Lloyd and I got down next morning. I said, "How'd you sleep?" which is just my way of saying good morning.

Momma said, "Didn't." She can snore all night and then next morning say she didn't close her eyes. "I kept hearing things. Doors opening, toilets flushing, floors creaking."

Lloyd stopped pouring his coffee. "Floors creaking?"

I had heard a little commotion myself, but it had seemed only natural with company in the house. I said, "Momma, don't do Lloyd this way."

She gave me an indignant look. "I would not do Lloyd any way but good," she said, "and you know it."

I said, "It was probably me. I had to get up. Twice."

Lloyd said, "Was the noise coming from the den?"

"I better not say or Jean will claim I'm doing something bad to you."

"Or was it coming from Sara's room?"

Momma put her index finger and thumb together and ran them across her lips. "Zip," she said. Lloyd went to scraping his nails.

"Honey," I said, "you're getting fingernail in your coffee."

Sara and Bobby spent the morning in the den, packing books and tapes. From the breeze-through where Momma and I sat doing some handwork, I could hear them chattering and laughing. Lloyd prowled through the house for a while, and then he could no longer resist looking in on Sara and Bobby. He went in the den and said, "I won't be interfering if I watch the television, will I?" He turned on a baseball game.

Bobby said, "Y'all come over to Atlanta and Sara and I'll take you to see the Braves in person."

The television went dead. Lloyd said, "I'm a football man myself." It is true he played football in high school, but he will watch any sport, including bowling if that's all that's on. He came out to the breeze-through and told me he was going out to the factory.

I said, "Saturday won't anybody be there, will there?"

"I'll be there, won't I?" he said. "I guess I'm still some-body." I followed him back into the house.

He got his Panama down from the hallway closet shelf and stood twirling it on his finger. "Why'd she bring him? We could have helped her pack."

I said, "Honey, you said yourself she's an adult now."

He twisted his shoulders at me. "If I've already said it, Jean, you don't have to say it again, do you?" That is the way with Lloyd. He is the best-natured man in the world, but he can get glum and pouty. He doesn't enjoy it the way Momma does, and if it doesn't get too far along, I can usually draw it out of him.

"I'll probably take a nap," I said. "I'm going to have to give up even the decaf, and you know I dearly love coffee."

"That really was you your momma heard?"

"Didn't I say it was?" He looked at me suspiciously, but Lloyd is the easiest man in the world to fib to because he so wants to believe you. I stretched and pretended to yawn. "I

won't be very helpful if Sara needs something. Are you sure
you have to go out there today?"

He thought a moment, and then he said, "I guess it isn't
polite to go off when we have company." He put his hat back
on the shelf.

For all the good staying home did him, he might as well have
spent the afternoon at the factory tending his pup tents and
toaster covers. Sara took Bobby off to see the sights. Lloyd got
so glum he spent most of the afternoon out in his workshop in
the garage, hammering and nailing. He says it makes him feel
better to make something, but all he seems to do is saw wood
apart and nail the pieces back together.

Sara and Bobby weren't home by our regular supper hour
which is six. I must have been a mind-reader because I had
fixed a cold supper that could wait.

Momma and Lloyd and I waited out on the porch. I said,
"Bobby seems a nice, friendly boy."

"Gawky," Lloyd said. He threw out the word as though it
indicated a kind of spiritual shortcoming or something terrible
like bad breath.

"So were you, Lloyd," Momma said. Then she laughed.
"But I guess what was good enough for my daughter isn't
good enough for yours."

"What does he do for a living, anyway?" Lloyd asked.

I said, "Sara says he's some kind of computer genius. He
does programming and stuff."

"Is that all he can do to support himself?"

Momma and I didn't say anything, and then we both
broke out laughing. I said, "You expect him to be a doctor and
a lawyer, too?" But Lloyd didn't see the fun in it.

About seven-fifteen, Sara and Bobby drove up. As they came
up the walk, Sara called, "I'm sorry we're so late. We drove all
the way to Auburn and back. You should have gone with us."

Lloyd said, "We didn't know we were invited."

Sara said, "And we didn't know we were going."

"You might have called to tell us you'd be late for dinner," Lloyd said. "But I guess that's not important."

Sara went to the back of his chair and put her arms around his neck. "If you start pouting," she said, "I'm going to hold my breath until I'm blue in the face."

Lloyd could not help smiling, though he obviously begrudged it.

"I'm starving," said Bobby. "Sara wouldn't let me have but one slice of pizza on the way home. She said I shouldn't take the edge off my appetite because you're the best cook in the world."

Sara had never said such a thing to me, and I wondered if he had made it up. He seemed to be the kind of boy who would invent things to make you happy.

Bobby offered to do the dishes. I said I was much obliged but he and Sara were on a holiday and oughtn't to work. After I cleaned up the kitchen, I joined the four others in the breezethrough. Sara was telling about her job at Brotherhood Life and her apartment. Momma asked if she had a good lock on the door.

Sara said, "I have a regular lock, a deadbolt, and a chain."

Bobby said, "And sometimes she jams a chair under the doorknob, Granny, then she sits in the chair all night."

"And I pray," said Sara.

Momma laughed. "You're such a heathen, the walls might come tumbling down if you prayed."

Bobby let out a yelp of laughter. I have never known a grown man to laugh so much, if grown he was. Momma smiled in that way that shows how pleased she is with herself.

Lloyd said, "I don't think Sara's safety is a laughing matter." Everybody looked at him, but he didn't look at anybody.

Finally I said, "I hear the Atlanta airport is mighty busy." So we talked about air travel for a while and then about traffic in general. Momma said trains were the best way to go if you had to go, and she told how wonderful our trip to visit Thad had been the year before. And then Sara said she was going to take Bobby down the street to show him off to her high school best friend.

As they walked down the walk, Bobby put his arm diagonally across Sara's back and stuck his big bony hand in the back pocket of her jeans, as easy as if that hip belonged to him. I heard Momma going "um-um" inside her throat, and as soon they turned the corner out of sight, she said, "I'm real sorry about your eyesight, Jean."

"What do mean, Momma?" I said, though I knew.

She said, "Well, you must not have seen where that boy put his hand or surely you would have said something."

I waved my hand in the air. "They're friends, Momma."

"My friends don't put their hands on my bottom," she said.

Lloyd stood up and said, "I'm going to bed." He thought for a moment and then flopped down again. "No. I'm staying up until they come home and settle for the night."

We moved into the den and turned on the television. Pretty soon Momma went to bed—she says Saturday is the worst shows in the week. Sara and Bobby came home about a half hour later. As soon as they walked in, Lloyd touched the remote to turn off the television.

"Beddybyes, everybody," he said, stretching.

Sara said, "In a while. I want some more of that strawberry short cake. You hungry, Bobby?"

"I'm always hungry," Bobby said.

Lloyd sat back down and turned the television back on. Sara looked at him and shook her head. Then she walked over to him, leaned down, and rested her chin on his head. "What're you watching?"

"I don't know," he muttered and remoted off the machine.

One of Lloyd's best talents is sleeping. I once told him if we were on an airplane and a terrorist took over, he would snooze all the way to Beirut. He said what was the point of staying awake when you weren't going to see anything you wanted to see.

But even after we heard Bobby slam the den door and Sara close hers, he just could not fall asleep. I could feel him every once in a while raise his down ear off the pillow and cock his head to listen. And then he would flop over on his other side and do the same. He didn't seem to figure out which was his best ear. Finally he turned on his back and smashed the pillow down to free both ears for listening. We lay there about five minutes without speaking, and then I said, "If we had put Bobby in Carl's room like I wanted instead of the den, you could put yourself to sleep watching television."

He said, "Maybe I can anyway. Maybe he isn't in the den."

"You think he moved into Carl's room?"

"Maybe he moved into *her* room," he said.

Sara and Bobby together in bed. I had thought about my children misbehaving and things like that, but I had never allowed myself to picture what that really was. Now for the first time I saw Sara and Bobby with their bodies doing what bodies do to make love. I've never much liked to think about people making love. It seems so undignified, even ludicrous. God should have invented a better way. I'm not claiming I don't like it myself, but it made me almost sick to picture my own daughter that way. You know it's going to happen, but you don't think it ever will. I knew it had.

To get the picture out of my head, I began to hum, though I don't think it was a real tune, just humming noise. "Don't try to tell me you're not worried, too," Lloyd said. "I hear you humming."

I said, "Honey, she's out of our jurisdiction now."

He thrashed around for a while and then said, "I just can't believe she would want to with that gawky boy."

If it was hard on a mother to think that way about a daughter, it was double hard on a father. Even if he thought it was the most natural thing in the world for everybody else, it

wouldn't be for his little girl, not yet, and not this man, whoever he was.

"We don't know that she does," I said. I wrapped my arms
around him and snuggled up to him. "Let's just try to get
some sleep."

After a few more bounces, he finally dozed off. And then
he slept as though he was at the bottom of the ocean. A gawky
boy falling halfway down the steps an hour later was not
enough to wake him. But I shot straight up in bed and
straight out into the darkened hall.

I switched on the light and there he was, his legs toward
me and his head toward Momma, standing in the doorway to
her room. He was wearing nothing but his underdrawers. Just
then Sara came out in her nightgown and robe and leaned
over the banister.

"I must have missed a step," Bobby said. He began to
laugh.

I expected Sara to laugh, too, but she didn't. She said,
"Shush," and put her finger to her lips. I looked down at
Momma. She looked up at me. Then she closed her door.

Sara gestured her head toward my room, her eyebrows
asking was Lloyd awake. I shook my head, and she gestured
me to go on back to bed. The boy didn't seem to be dead, so I
decided to let Sara tend him. What would I have said to them
anyway?

When I got back in bed, Lloyd mumbled, "What?"

I said, "Go on back to sleep." But after the house quieted,
I lay there for a half hour, so wide awake I could have heard a
mosquito buzzing in the kitchen.

Early Sunday morning we had a sweet rain shower, and by the
time I woke, everything had cooled off and freshened up.
During my wakeful time I had decided it would be better not
to tell Lloyd what had happened until after Sara and Bobby
left. Lloyd might say some things he would regret, and the
hurt feelings might be hard to heal. So while Lloyd showered

and dressed, I hurried downstairs to try to persuade Momma to go along. She was sitting in the breakfast nook, and Sara was leaning against the refrigerator. I could tell they had been at each other.

Sara looked over at me in a sheepish way and said, "I'm sorry we woke you last night."

I said, "I bet you are." The image of her and Bobby in bed flashed through my mind, but I squelched it as quick as I could.

"I guess Daddy is taking it pretty hard."

Before I could answer, Momma was talking. "You might have thought of that before. But I've already told you what I think about your shenanigans, and I won't say another word. But even your generation must know that some things are right and some are wrong."

"Yes, but we don't necessarily agree with yours on which is which," Sara said. "And when you're a grown-up you have to make your own decisions."

"And that makes everything all right?" Momma asked in her quick little voice. "Suppose a grown-up decides to murder?"

"Sometimes people can be so aggravated they can't help it." Sara glowered at Momma. Just listening, you would have thought they were twins.

"Lloyd will be down in a minute," I said to Momma. "He doesn't yet know what happened, and I've decided not to tell him until after Sara and Bobby leave. That'll be better for everybody. Now, Momma, I know your feelings on the subject, but please don't say anything for now."

Momma shot Sara a can-you-believe-your-ears look. "Lloyd didn't do anything wrong," she said, "so why are you planning to punish him? I never punished your daddy telling him all your shenanigans. Keep it to yourself."

Before I could respond, Lloyd walked in. He said good morning to everybody and slid into the breakfast nook alongside Momma. He sat there for a minute scraping his thumbnail over his fingernails. Then he turned to face Momma and in a nervous voice asked, "Well, how did you sleep last night?"

"Like an egg under a roosting hen," Momma said. "Jean must not have been tap-dancing through the house in the middle of the night."

Lloyd began to laugh, and he laughed so hard I just had to join in and so did Sara and Momma. People hearing us would have thought they had wandered into a lunatic asylum.

Bobby yelled from the den, "If anything is funny, save it. I'mo be out in a minute."

Sara and Bobby were to leave right after breakfast, and everybody was relieved that the visit was about over. I fixed my famous homemade buttermilk pancakes, this time with blackberries. Bobby said he didn't think anything so good could yet be so wholesome. He ate twenty-three. Lloyd tried to keep up, but he had to surrender after fifteen.

Ecuador

MOMMA came home from her Tuesday afternoon garden club pretending to be trying to hide her smile. I didn't want to disappoint her, so I fell right into her net. "What is it? The preacher getting a divorce?"

"The preacher getting a divorce!" she cried. "Don't keep me on tenterhooks. Who's the woman?" Momma will have her fun, but it can be exasperating.

"Okay," I said, "tell me what you're laughing at. Just say."

She flapped her hand at me. "Now, don't nag, Jean. I'll tell in my own good time."

Her own good time came when Lloyd got home at six and we were eating supper in the breakfast nook. She said, "Linwood Butterfield is in town."

She had not said that name to me in twenty-eight years. I carefully set my fork down on my plate. "That so?" I said. I glanced at Lloyd. He was staring at his plate, as though he was trying to decide exactly which lima bean he ought to eat next.

"Jean, you forgot my Dr. Scholl's pads again Saturday," Momma said. "If I don't have my Dr. Scholl's, I get this hurting like a tiny man hiding in my shoe is sticking a little knife in my fourth toe right where it grows out of the ball of my foot? Lloyd, have you ever had a really sharp pain in your foot when you have your shoes on and you can't grab it and make it stop?"

"No'm," Lloyd mumbled. He still hadn't located the bean he wanted.

I said, "I put the pads in your medicine cabinet as usual."

"How was I supposed to know that? You should have told me. Not that I'm not grateful for all you do for me, but still I did have to ask Lydia to stop at the drug store when I thought you hadn't done it. I certainly did not want to have to ask you again. That would have been nagging."

"Quit teasing, Momma. Where did you see Lin?"

Momma sighed and looked hard at me. "I'm trying to tell you if you will just give me a minute without interrupting. When he heard the girl at the drugstore say my name, he limped right over and told me who he was."

I said, "Limped?"

Lloyd said, "He broke his leg real bad in the rodeo back then."

I said, "You never told me that."

He said, "You never asked."

Momma laughed. "Good one, Lloyd."

None of us spoke for a minute, and then I said, "Where's he staying? I'm going to invite him for dinner. I mean, he is our cousin."

Momma looked as if I had tricked her. Lloyd stared down at his plate some more and said, "No harm done, I guess.

Actually, Linwood Butterfield is only my third cousin, although some folks call it second cousin once removed. I did not know him until the summer after Lloyd and I got engaged. His daddy, Momma's first cousin, had gone off to Texas to seek his fortune. Momma said Cousin Buddy was the only man in Texas with a pitchfork who hadn't made a million dollars in the oil business. He was doomed to be a pauper, she said. I didn't know that part of the family until Lin came with the rodeo to Florala when I was visiting my Butterfield cousins. And I'll just say it: we fell in love.

There is no point in trying to figure out how that could happen when I was already in love with Lloyd. I wasn't dissatisfied with Lloyd. Nobody could have been nicer than he was then and as it happens nobody could be a better husband. Maybe it was just Lin's wonderful golden color and the clean lines of his face. Or maybe it was because he made me laugh so hard and carefree at his stories about the rodeo and Alaska where he had mostly grown up.

Every day that week, I took the Greyhound to wherever the rodeo was—once as far away as Eufaula—and I sat in the stands. Lin wouldn't let them open the gate until he saw where I was sitting and he had waved his hat at me. Then he came out on his little quarter horse, a big grin on his face, twirling his lasso, and then off the horse and onto the bull and twisting and turning its horns and wrestling the bull to the ground until it lay like dead and me screaming until no sound was left to come.

When the rodeo was done each day, Lin drove me back to Jimmy Lee's, and we walked through the alfalfa down to the pond and sat on the bank. As dusk fell we watched the silver minnows glide along the edge. And when he touched my hair or my ear or my hand, something in my shook loose and I felt a way I'd never felt before.

After a week around the towns in South Alabama, the rodeo went on into Georgia. I took the bus to Montgomery where Lloyd had set up his little pup tent factory after he got back from the army. It was in a rickety old barn and Lloyd was up to his hair line in wood dust from the tent posts.

When I told him I couldn't marry him because I had fallen in love with Lin, he wiped his hands down his sides and said he understood that was just natural because everybody wants to break off at the last minute and he probably would himself as the time got closer. He said I was so smart I had invented a good reason but he was so dumb he couldn't understand it. When I said then he had to take it on faith, he laughed and said you could not force faith if it wasn't there. He kept laughing as though it was the best joke he'd heard in a long time.

I gave up arguing and went on to Birmingham to tell Momma. That was almost harder than telling Lloyd. She just looked at me for a while, as though too astonished to speak.

"So you told Lloyd you'd marry him when you didn't love him," she declared.

"I do love him," I said, "but this is different. Lin makes me feel alive."

"Alive isn't everything," she said. "A son of Buddy Butterfield is bound to be trouble, always looking for excitement, bouncing from flower to flower like a bee. You can't trust him, Jean." Then she gave me a long look. "You haven't done anything bad, have you? So you'd have to marry him?"

We hadn't. When we lay down on the grass at the edge of Jimmy Lee's pond, it was almost more than I could do to stop myself and him, but all we did was hold and kiss and touch. I had held us back because I believed it would taint us if we did anything before I had freed myself from Lloyd.

I said, "You raised me better than that."

In a real quiet voice, she said, "Did I raise you to make a promise and then break it and the heart of the finest man in the world? And mine, too?" And then the phone rang. It was Lloyd. All the joking had gone out of him, and he was crying.

All the rest of the summer, Lin kept sending me postcards to tell me the next town the rodeo would be in so I could join him. Somebody must have told him when I got married that fall—a card in early September postmarked Roanoke, Virginia, was the last I ever got.

The three of us never spoke his name again, but over the years, I often woke up thinking about him, looking into his dark eyes, tasting his special taste in my mouth, the pond like black glass in front of us, the smell of mown alfalfa surrounding us, and I lay there quivering. It's funny to get older and older and yet feel yourself the same as you were then. I'd reach out and touch Lloyd, still and silent beside me, and I'd feel the warmth of his back against my breasts as I drew myself tight against him.

The night Lin was coming for dinner, Lloyd got home at five-fifteen, forty-five minutes before he usually did, and he went straight upstairs. I could hear him splashing in the shower although I knew for a fact he had bathed that very morning. He came down freshly shaved and wearing a fresh shirt and a necktie. I hugged him and said, "Sometimes I think you are the biggest fool in the world."

When the doorbell rang, Lloyd got up so quick the bell was still echoing when he opened the door. "You must be Cousin Linwood," he shouted, as though warning us that an unexpected and unwelcome guest had arrived. Lloyd kind of dragged Lin into the living room, pulling on his arm, as though he was an MC making a bashful somebody take a bow.

For a long moment, Lin looked from me to Momma to me to Momma, smiling shyly and us smiling back. He had fluffy gray sideburns and he was nearly bald and his face was as cracked and stained as old cowhide. He held a box out to Momma. "I brought you some chocolate-covered cherries, Cousin Clara," he said, shooting me a quick look.

One evening he had brought me a box of chocolate-covered cherries. We had taken it down to the pond with us, but the candy was so chewy we could hardly separate our jaws once we had bit into it. So we dropped it piece by piece into the water. Seeing catfish eating chocolate-covered cherries seemed to us the funniest thing in the world, and we laughed so hard we almost fell in the pond. Knowing he had remembered that, I felt my eyes cloud over and my heart drop into my belly. What could be more foolish, I said to myself, than a woman my age reacting like a teenager.

Momma gave me a sharp look and took the box from Lin as though it was a little too hot to handle. "Aren't you nice," she finally managed to say.

Lloyd grinned and smacked his lips. "Open it and let's have a piece."

Momma said, "My goodness, Lloyd, we don't want to ruin our appetite when we'll be eating so soon, do we?"

Lloyd sat down and seemed to collapse. He said, "I don't

have any appetite." Then he straightened up and laughed and winked as though what he had meant was he could eat a side of beef all by himself.

You have to give it to Momma: she has such a strong social sense that she can be friendly even if she doesn't like you. "Well, Linwood," she said, nodding him toward a chair, "have a seat and tell us the story of your life."

Lin smiled. "I don't believe you'd find it edifying, Cousin Clara. I'm a rolling stone. Been everywhere from Hollywood to Khartoum."

"What do you call what you do for a living?" Momma asked.

"Real bad." Lin laughed. Or I should say he giggled. The sound hit me hard, for I remembered how that deep voice of his could suddenly turn to a giggle that sounded like a girl's. I felt a hitch in my breath, and I stood up.

"Never had a family?" Momma asked.

Lin glanced at me. "Two wives but no children. No wife now."

"So," Momma said, nodding, "you're a soldier of fortune."

"I'd say misfortune," Lin said. He glanced at me again. "But I won't deny it's been fun."

I said, "I'll get dinner on the table."

"Now, Lin," Momma said, "don't expect Jean to compete with the fancy cooks in what-was-that-foreign-country-you-said? You'll just have to be satisfied with plain food."

"Always been my favorite," he said.

Lloyd usually says his piece and no more. But he monopolized the entire conversation the first fifteen minutes of dinner. He told how he had been a real soldier in the first days of Vietnam and had spent eight months in Okinawa and gone to Tokyo for his R&R. He said he went to a swimming pool and got a naked massage from a Japanese lady.

Momma said, "I don't think you ought to be telling that kind of thing on yourself, Lloyd. Please change the subject."

Lloyd is accommodating. He began to tell about how he got started in business. Momma and I had heard the story a hundred times, but we listened out of politeness. He told about saving his army pay despite the Japanese lady, setting up in a barn to make pup tents, and ten years later building a little factory and adding toaster covers.

He put his face up kind of close to Lin's. "I now have twenty-three employees and looking for more."

Momma laughed. "I don't believe Linwood is after a job, Lloyd."

"And I'm not offering him one," Lloyd said. "You need steady workers if you don't want a lot of returns." He stopped. "I don't mean to say you're not steady. I mean...."

"Now it's my turn to say please change the subject," Lin said, ducking his head. "You're cutting too close to the bone." He giggled again, and we all laughed.

After that, Momma took over. She cannot resist an attentive audience, and Lin was a good one. She ran down the list of all the relatives, telling who was alive and who was dead and who did what and why. She didn't even hold back on the scandals. She told how Cousin Pelham had invented an electric fingernail clipper, but when he was demonstrating it to a company that might want to buy it, he cut off the tip of his little finger. When that got a big laugh from Lin, she was satisfied enough to quit. She said, "Now it's your turn to tell about Buddy's folks."

Lin said, "I can't make up yarns the way you do, Cousin Clara. I guess I'll have to tell the truth, unfortunate as it is." We were at dessert by then—a peach cobbler from peaches I had canned the previous summer. Lin said after Cousin Buddy went bankrupt in Texas, he moved the family to California, then to Arizona, and then to run a hotel in Cape Yakataga, Alaska. "I believe he aims to be in the *Guinness Book of Records* for going bankrupt in every state in the union," Lin said.

"Is he still good-looking?" Momma asked. "Has he aged

well?"

"I don't know you'd say that. He's bald and stooped, but he still moves quick as a fly."

"Quick-tongued, too," Momma said. "Talk anybody into almost anything."

Lin laughed. "He could talk bankers into lending him money, but he never could talk them out of foreclosing."

Momma said. "Tell us about the rest of the family."

Then Lin told us that his sister Lana was married to an FBI agent and they had just moved to Chicago from the nation's capitol. He said his brother Ernest was a forest ranger in Montana in the summertime and a hand on a fishing boat in the Gulf of Mexico in the winter.

I said, "That sounds like an interesting life."

Momma shot me a look. "Your family seems mighty flighty. Nobody stays put for long."

Lin laughed and shook his head. "No moss grows, that's a fact. Speaking of moss, I better get moving. If you tell me where the phone is, I'll call my friend Henry to come get me. He brought me here. Remember Henry, Jean, from the rodeo?" That was the first mention of those times.

I said, "Smoked cigars and spat a lot?"

"The same. Gave up cigars, still spits a lot." We both laughed, and I could see the pleasure in his eyes.

Lloyd said, "We won't hear of you calling somebody else when we have two fine cars in the driveway. I'll take you." He looked at me and then at Momma and then at Lin. Then he sighed. "No, I guess it's my turn to do the dishes. Jean, will you drive Cousin Linwood wherever?"

Lin shook hands with Lloyd and Lloyd patted him on the back and called him Cousin Linwood a few more times. Lin turned to Momma and said how fine she looked.

Momma said, "I feel just stifled in the house tonight, even if it is only March. I believe I'll ride with you, Jean, to get some fresh air."

∾

The next morning at ten, Lin called me.

He said, "I counted the number of words you said last night and it totaled seventeen."

I had to laugh. "When Momma's around...."

"That's what I'm calling about. How about us talking when Momma's not around? Like over lunch?"

I was so taken aback all I could think to say was, "I don't believe I can."

"Lloyd would mind?"

"Of course not. Why would he?" I knew my voice was what you'd call defensive, and that was the wrong tone. "Where'd you have in mind?"

We set up a time and place to meet, and then I called Lloyd. I told him Lin had invited me for lunch. When he didn't say anything for a good minute, I said, "You don't mind, do you?"

"What's to mind?" he said. Then he laughed. "I've got a date myself. With a salesman wants to sell me some fancy new rickrack for the toaster covers."

When I told Momma, she said, "Why go to a restaurant and spend money? We have that pot roast from last night."

I said, "There's no harm having lunch with a cousin."

She glowered for a moment. Then she said, "I hope you won't be gone long because I want you to drive me somewhere this afternoon."

"Where?"

"The drug store." She started to walk off. "Of course I can walk if I stop two or three times to rest."

The place I met Lin wasn't so much a restaurant as a road house on the Greenville road. Henry had claimed it had the best shrimp in central Alabama, fresh out of the Gulf, and he wasn't far wrong. Lin and I sat across from each other in a rickety wooden booth, as far from the blaring juke as we could get. As soon as we sat down, Lin leaned across the splintery table and said, "Say true: how are you, Jean?"

And I said, "Fine."

He threw himself back against the booth. "That makes eighteen words I've heard now."

I said, "Sometimes one word tells better than a whole bunch."

And then neither of us had anything to say until the waitress walked up. She must have been carrying two hundred and fifty pounds on five feet and two inches. She had on a pink shimmery tent-like dress that hung from her shoulders, and she was wearing a big pink ribbon in her hair. I thought, Well, she's done the best she can for herself as is. She handed us two menus that looked as if they had been soaked in beer and smeared with grape jelly, and then she just stood there.

Lin said, "Give us a minute."

"Take all the time you want," the waitress said. "I'll just stand here. Fact is, it's a lot easier for me to stand so my fat hangs mostly off my shoulders. When I have to walk, my fat swings and pulls my bones every which of a way. That's what tires fat people. It uses up a lot of energy to keep everything under control."

I looked at Lin and he looked at me. His face began to jitter and quake. I knew I was on the verge myself, and I dropped my head close to the menu as though I was shortsighted. Finally, I felt able to mutter, "Shrimp cocktail, cole slaw, ice tea."

In a choked voice, Lin said, "Same."

When she was out of earshot, we both broke up laughing, even though it wasn't very nice to do. After that, talking was easy. He told me funny stories about being in the Sudan and Thailand and Uruguay. He said his next trip was to Ecuador. I said he sure lived an exciting life, and he said yes, but it was lonely. I asked if he was in the CIA, and he laughed and said, "Not likely." But he didn't say what he did do.

When the waitress brought us our shrimp and tea and he was busy eating, I got up the nerve to ask him how he hurt his leg. He said he had taken a hard spill when the rodeo was in

West Virginia. He said it was just recklessness had caused the accident, because he hadn't much cared about being alive. I didn't know what to say, so I didn't say anything.

Then he put his little fork on the plate and shook his head. "You always could make me talk more than I should. I want to know more about you."

I said, "I'm fine," and we both laughed.

But then I did talk a little. I told him that Carl was in construction, working in Mobile, and Sara was in insurance in Atlanta. When he asked who they took after, I said Sara took after Momma and Carl took after Lloyd.

"Does it make you sad for nobody to take after you?"

I said, "I like to have different types of people around, and I always have me around."

"I wish I did," he said. "I been wishing that a long time."

I felt the heat rise up my throat. "You shouldn't talk like that," I said.

"Remember how I couldn't start until I spotted where you were sitting?"

I said, "All of us have might-have-beens."

"What's yours?"

After a minute, I said, "Well, you." Then I felt so nervous I jumped up and said, "It's nearly three-thirty. I was supposed to take Momma somewhere."

"Jean," he said, but I was already walking across the dance floor.

He left some money on the table and caught up with me at the door. We walked side by side to my car. Every time he came down on his good leg, his arm brushed mine. Once he stumbled and, to steady himself, he rested his hand on my shoulder. When we got to the car, he said, "Kissing kin," and he kissed me. I felt just as I had when we were young and sitting on the pond bank and the something inside shaking loose.

I opened the car door, but he put his arm across so I couldn't get inside. "Lunch tomorrow," he said. "I won't let you leave unless you promise. What's the harm, Jean?"

I thought, Well, I can say I will just so he'll close the door. And so I said yes.

At home I found a note on the kitchen table from Momma: "Forgot I had canasta."

When Lloyd came home he hung his fedora in the hall closet and came to the kitchen to give me my hello-kiss. He said, "Well, did you have fun with your cousin?" When I said we had gone to a real fine lunch place on the highway, he slapped his hands together. "Good. Fine. I'm glad you went." He stood there grinning, waiting, but I didn't have more to say.

I fixed pork chops with applesauce—one of Lloyd's favorites—for dinner and Lloyd said they were the best ever. Momma said the chops might be a tad too dry. Lloyd said that might be good because maybe dry pork chops had less cholesterol. Momma said she could remember way back before anybody had ever had cholesterol so they didn't have any choice but to die of old age.

Talk went on like that for about ten minutes, and then Momma said, "Cat got your tongue, Jean? Tell us about your lunch."

"I had shrimp," I said. "Does it have much cholesterol?"

Momma squirmed her body and pursed her lips. "I mean, how was Linwood?"

"About the same as last night." I looked at Lloyd. "He wants me to have lunch again tomorrow."

Momma slapped her hands together. "Surely you won't. Lloyd?"

"It's up to Jean," Lloyd said. Then he ducked his head and looked at his hands. He began to scrape his thumbnail over his other nails. Nobody said anything else, but I didn't see Lloyd's eyes again all evening.

Momma and I stayed up to watch *NYPD Blue*, Momma's favorite show though she said the men were brutes and fools and the women were hussies and fools and the show ought to have been banned from the air.

When the show was over and I stood up, Momma said, "Jean, I have something I want to say to you."

I said, "Just this once, don't say a word."

I went upstairs, got undressed in the dark, and crawled in beside Lloyd. I was so tense I couldn't sleep. He's just my cousin, I said to myself. The other is over.

Lloyd was turned away from me on his side, but by the way he breathed I knew he wasn't asleep. I snuggled up close to his warm back and put my arm around him and began to play with the hair on his chest. Then I pushed my knee between his thighs.

I whispered, "Lloyd honey."

He said, "I don't put out fires I don't start."

I pulled back from him. "I can't believe you said that."

He muttered, "I can't either, but I did. I'm sorry."

That's all we said. He finally went to sleep, but I kept thinking of Lin and how he had kissed me. Then I thought, Don't I have a right to feel alive? Church on Sunday and bridge on Wednesday and two weeks vacation at Pompano Beach or Pensacola. Pensacola? Why not Ecuador?

That was the idea I got caught on. I don't know a thing about Ecuador except it's in South America, but it sounded like immense dark mountains and thick forests and people with bright eyes and golden skin. I lulled myself to sleep saying the word over and over. Ecuador.

Nobody mentioned Lin at breakfast the next morning. Lloyd gave me his usual goodbye-kiss, but he still hadn't looked me in the eye. I could see talk bristling on Momma's face, and so as quick as I could I went out to the yard to count the drunken snails that had drowned in my pans of beer.

I heard the telephone ring, and then Momma came to the kitchen steps and called my name. I wouldn't let her catch my eye as I ran past her into the kitchen

Lin said, "Yesterday was like twenty-eight years had never happened, wasn't it?" My heartbeat quickened and a little sweat began to bead on my forehead.

I said, "It was wonderful."

He said, "Same time, same place, same wonderful."

"Twelve-thirty?" I said into the phone.

From the doorway, Momma said, "There's a Lin or a Buddy for every woman, but we don't let it ruin a good life. I didn't let Buddy ruin mine."

I silently said, Ecuador, and I tried to picture me and Lin against the forest with a fire burning in it and us surrounded by dark smiling people who kind of glowed. But the word had lost its magic. I got to thinking that Ecuador was probably just another poverty-stricken country trying to get rich on drugs. And I knew I would never go there, wouldn't want to, even, except maybe when I lay awake on lonely evenings. Maybe just having those evenings would be enough.

I said, "I'm not coming, Lin."

He said, "Don't I at least get a face-to-face rejection this time?"

After a pause, I said, "I better hang up."

"Then hang up," Momma shrieked in a whisper, right into my ear. I hadn't known she was behind me and her voice shocked me so I slammed down the phone.

She came around in front of where I was sitting. I said, "Buddy?"

She shrugged. "As you see, I survived." She put her hand under my chin to lift it. "And I can see you're going to be all right, too."

I said I'd be just fine.

Brotherly Love

According to Aunt Rosa, when Momma and her brother Buzz were little, sometimes they were as close as two eggs scrambled in a skillet. If one started a thought, the other spoke it. If one fell in the pond, the other almost died. If one did mischief, they both got whipped. Other times they were like chickens pecking after the same corn kernel. Aunt Rosa told me Buzz bloodied Momma's nose and she cut him on the arm with a butcher knife. Once Momma teased Buzz so bad he tied her up in the barn for a whole day right next to where their old horse had done its business, and that night she put the business in his shoes. They were like that even when they were grown and lived in different towns, Momma in Birmingham then and Buzz in Talledega then and now. They'd visit or telephone every week or they'd squabble and not speak for months. Then they really fell out and didn't speak for three years.

It happened about six months after Rosa passed. Rosa never married, and Buzz and Momma and my aunt Jenny were the heirs. When Buzz finally sold the old Butterfield place in Demopolis, where they had all grown up, they came together to pick over the spoils, such as they were. Momma and I drove to Demopolis, and Buzz picked up Jenny in Sylacauga and drove her and his daughter-in-law, Edwina, down in his Cadillac car.

We walked around the house, figuring out what Rosa had

left that was worth taking. "Look at her," Momma whispered, motioning toward Edwina, who was examining the silver ladle with the letter "B" engraved on it. The family claimed it was the only thing Great-great-grandmother Butterfield had kept from the Yankees. "Must think that thing is worth money. She's as greedy as an old sow."

The three heirs drew straws to see who would pick first, and Momma won. I had my eye on the love seat where the two people sat side by side but facing in opposite directions with an arm rest between so they couldn't get at each other. It was a real conversation piece and would have looked wonderful in my front hall. But Momma said it was too big for the front hall.

When Momma chose the ladle, Buzz gave her a hard look and nodded to Edwina. She pointed at the maple chiffonier that had once been Momma's. Jenny chose the love seat. It took about a half hour for the three of them to make their choices and decide what to leave for the junkman.

While Jenny made ice tea, the rest of us took chairs out to where the two halls made a cross in the center of the house. Those halls were open at the ends, and the wind whipped through going ninety miles an hour even if not a leaf moved outside. Aunt Rosa was pretty set in her ways. and all she had been willing to change in the old place was to put in an AEK.

The minute we got settled, Edwina gave Buzz a nudge, and he leaned toward Momma. "Since I'm the only one has a Butterfield line still going, I thought the family would want me to have the ladle."

Momma said, "Thad still has a B-line going. It could just as well be for Blaine."

That caused me a twinge of jealousy because Thad was always Momma's pet. He is six years older than I, and hard as I tried I could never catch up with him. He and I had never been close. When I was in my early teens, I thought he might not even recognize me if he saw me downtown in a crowd of girls. We have never been like Momma and Buzz.

I said, "But it's for Butterfield. Wouldn't it be cheating to say it was for Blaine?"

"Nobody will know the difference," Momma said.

Edwina looked as though a flare had gone off in her head. "Why, I bet Poppa would trade you the chiffonier and the gate-leg table both for it." She fluttered her eyelids. "Two selections for one. I know Poppa wouldn't keep that chiffonier from you, knowing it was yours once."

Momma laughed. "I couldn't wait for Rosa to die before I had a place to store my clothes, so I bought another one about fifty years ago. And I never thought gate-legs were reliable." She winked at me where nobody could see. "I'm content with my ladle, and since you're a widower leading a bachelor life, Buzz, you don't need a ladle."

"Of course I don't need one," said Buzz, flapping his hand. "I want it as a present for Edwina. Girl's got her heart set on it. How much will you sell it for? Fifty dollars? A hundred?"

"Sell a family heirloom? For money?" Momma put on her outraged look. "I would never ever."

Buzz slapped both his hips real hard. "Then keep the damn ladle."

Edwina reached over and touched his knee. "But, Poppa...." she began, but he slapped his hips again.

"I won't hear another word about it, so hush," he said, Edwina fell back in her chair.

Jenny said, "I'll miss this old place." She was always the peacemaker.

Buzz jerked around at her. "I won't, not a whit. I'm glad to be shed of it."

Momma smiled. "It sure is cool in the summer."

Buzz said, "My home is completely air-conditioned."

Momma said, "I couldn't breathe in one of those infernal machines, sucking up all the fresh air and spitting back sour."

Buzz said, "That's just your opinion."

Momma smiled sweetly. "Who's else would I express?"

Jenny said, "Now y'all be sweet."

"I'm being sweet," Momma said. "Buzz is just mad because he didn't get the ladle. He thinks being the brother he has the right to anything he wants."

Buzz turned so red you could see the flush through his pale pink hair. He leaned forward and shouted, "I'll tell you what the brother has a right to. It's the eight percent real estate commission for selling this place."

Momma looked at me to show she didn't believe her ears. "You don't get a commission for selling this place. What's the executor for if not to sell the property?"

"If you understood one thing about business you'd know the executor oversees everything and I've done that. The real estate man sees to the selling and gets eight percent. And I was the real estate man. I made four trips down from Talledega before I could locate a buyer."

Momma's eyes flared. "You don't have a right to a penny more than your one-third."

"I have a right to my one-third plus eight percent, and I'm going to take it."

I was pretty sure Buzz was just talking—he has plenty of money and he's always been generous—so I motioned Momma to calm down. But she wouldn't be stopped.

"So you're going to cheat your two widowed sisters. I'm sorry to live to this day."

"Oh, Sister, it can't be much," Jenny said. "What's the point of fussing over a tad of money?"

Momma gave her a pitying look. She has always thought Jenny was a step slow. "I'm not greedy, but I won't be bullied and I won't be cheated."

Jenny went to work on Buzz. "If Sister feels so strong about it, why don't you just take the eight percent off mine and yours?"

Momma threw me a can-you-believe-your-ears look. "He wouldn't be taking it from himself, Jenny—he'd be *giving* it. He'd only be stealing it from you."

"I am not stealing," Buzz shouted, slamming his foot to the floor. "I am taking what's mine. It's the principle of the thing."

Momma slapped that one away. "The only principle is you want more money. You always loved money too much, but you won't have any of mine."

Buzz lumbered to his feet. He seemed to swell up taller and stouter. "I'll take it out of your share before I make out your check."

Momma stood up, too, but she only came to Buzz's shoulder. "We'll see what the judge has to say about that."

Jenny gasped. "Oh, Sister, you wouldn't take family into a court of law? That would break my heart." She brought out one of the embroidered linen handkerchiefs she always has stuffed in the front of her dress, and she put her face in it and began to wail.

"See what you've done," Momma said to Buzz. She went over to Jenny and patted her shoulder. "I didn't say I'd do it. I said I could if I wanted to." She looked at Buzz. "I was teasing you, Burt Butterfield, and I was going to give you the ladle. But now you could stake me to an eight-foot ant hill and I wouldn't give it up."

"That's fine with me. I didn't want it in the first place. I'd a heap rather have the eight percent. Edwina, get your hat."

Within five minutes, we had all driven away from the old house where they had learned how to be brother and sister.

If it hadn't been for Jenny, we would have lost touch with the Buzz side of the family. Jenny told us when Buzz sold his hardware stores in Talledega and Sylacauga and when Burt Junior and Edwina had moved in with Buzz to take care of him and when his daughter Carmen's husband became a city councilman.

"I miss the old coot," Momma said. "Nobody could ever make me laugh as much as he could. Or cry either. Losing your brother is a terrible thing. I feel like I've come untwined and I'm just hanging loose. Jean, I hope you never have such a falling out with Thad."

I said she didn't need to worry since we had never been twined tight enough to notice any loosening.

When the check for Momma's share of Rosa's estate came, no eight percent had been deducted. I asked Momma if she was now going to make it up with Buzz, but she said, "I am of a forgiving nature, but not a do-it-first nature."

After nearly three years, we received a letter from Edwina saying that Buzz wanted to make peace with everybody he was on the outs with, and if Momma thought that included her, he would come to see her. Edwina would drive him down if we would but name the day and the hour.

As I read her the letter, Momma's eyes gleamed. "He should be ashamed of himself to have let this thing go on so long." She stared at me, daring me to speak the obvious. I didn't. Her face softened. "I'm big enough to admit some of it may have been my doing."

"Well, that's a start," I said.

They were to arrive at two or so and then drive back home before dark. Momma had her hair set and nails done that morning and then fretted all the way through lunch for fear she might mess up her manicure. I brought home some flowers to brighten up the living room, and she worked over them until there was hardly a petal left. She claims to love flowers, but she acts as though she's trying to murder them. I always have to stick some green in the bare spots and twist broken stems around each other so they won't droop.

We were both dressed and ready by one-thirty and went out to the breeze-through to wait. Momma pretended to crochet, but she took out more stitches than she put in. Finally she just let the yarn drop to her lap.

She said, "Did you know I gave him his name? I couldn't say Burt." She smiled. "He was such a sweet boy. We used to go to the Saturday picture show in Demopolis. We didn't have talkies in those days, and he'd read me the writing under the pictures even though he could hardly read himself." She tried a few more stitches. "Now, Jean, let bygones be bygones. I'd appreciate it if you didn't mention what happened."

At two on the dot, a big red Cadillac drew up in front of our house. Edwina got out and went around to open the door of the passenger seat. Buzz dropped his feet to the curb and grabbed the roof edge to pull himself out. As he stood on the curb getting his breath, his enormous belly made his legs look like a duck's.

Momma whispered, "She's trying to kill him, letting him get so fat."

She opened the screen door and called, "Yoohoo," and they looked up and waved. We hurried down the steps. Momma and Buzz grinned at each other a minute or two and then reached and hugged and kissed. When they stood back, their eyes were moist, and so were mine.

Momma pecked the air beside Edwina's cheek, and I did the same. I hardly recognized Edwina. At Rosa's she had been dumpy and soft, but now she looked like somebody who spent a lot of energy not eating. And she had turned her thinnish hair the color of dishwater into a thick head of copper-red curls.

Momma said, "Jean, surely you don't expect the folks to stand out on the sidewalk all afternoon, do you?"

We started up the walk, Momma in front and me in the rear. Edwina held Buzz's elbow and they staggered along. It was a struggle. With each step he set his cane forward, lifted a leg after it, and then rolled his belly in the same direction. Every step or two Edwina laughed, a kind of unpleasant sound as though she had a thick wall blocking her nose.

Once we got to the living room, Buzz sat down in the first chair he reached. The chair groaned, but it held. Momma drew up another chair close by, and the two of them smiled at each other for a full minute. I knew Momma did not want to say what she was thinking, and I knew she would say it. She said, "How much do you weigh, Buzz?"

Buzz bellowed out a big laugh and stomped his cane in the rug. "Didn't I say that'd be the first thing she'd talk about?" he said to Edwina. "I make a point of not knowing my weight, Clara. I don't want to ruin the last pleasure God and Edwina allow me."

"It's best to age a little drier," Momma said.

Buzz shook his head. "I believe in being full of juice right up to the end so when they slice me open they'll think it's a big ripe watermelon full of seeds." Momma and Buzz thought that was pretty funny, and they laughed for a minute or two.

"I been starving to death since we left Talledega," Buzz said, "but this girl gets behind the wheel of my Cadillac and it would take the entire Alabama Highway Patrol to stop her. You'd be surprised how determined a little bit of a thing like Edwina can be."

"Jean can take a hint," Momma said.

I went to the kitchen and got the pitcher of ice tea from the refrigerator and the plate of cheese and crackers I had already set out and the two cakes I'd baked, one chocolate and one carrot, in case Edwina or Buzz was allergic. Buzz cut off a big hunk of cheese and grabbed a fistful of crackers. Edwina just took tea, after making sure it wasn't sweetened.

Momma said, "I was just reminiscing with Jean, Buzz. Remember how you read me the lines at the picture show? I always loved you for that."

Buzz smiled. "Buck Jones was my hero. Yours was Tim Maynard."

"Tim was better looking," Momma said.

"Buck sat a horse better," Buzz said.

"Tim was the best rider," Momma said.

"You're wrong," Buzz said.

Edwina said, "Now, just stop it, y'all. Let's not quarrel."

Momma gave her a scorching look, but Edwina didn't

seem to notice. Momma turned back to Buzz. "Remember practicing on that old mule we had? Ben? These girls don't know what they've missed, not having an old mule to ride."

Edwina said, "I'd rather have my Cadillac."

Momma gave her another scorching look. "Ben was more fun to ride than a Cadillac car, no matter who really owns the car. Wasn't he, Buzz?" Edwina just smiled and leaned back in her chair.

Momma and Buzz began talking about Ben and another mule named Bill and some boys on the next farm who drove their Daddy's Model T into the creek and a cousin who gave herself a perm and went bald and a trick Buzz played on Momma and a trick Momma played to get even. I cut Buzz a big slice of chocolate cake, and he motioned me for a piece of carrot cake as well. He ate them both without stopping the talk. And he and Momma laughed until I feared for their hearts, Momma slapping Buzz's knee, Buzz pounding his cane into my new blue rug.

Then Edwina jumped right into the middle. "It like to have killed me and Poppa when you all fell out."

"It's over," said Momma. "We don't need to talk about it."

"But we've just been miserable until we could come down and make it up with you."

Momma laughed. "I been here every day except the two weeks each summer Lloyd takes us on a vacation."

Edwina ignored that. "Poppa loves you so much, Aunt Clara, he'd give you just about anything you wanted."

Momma said, "Buzz is the first Butterfield ever had a nickel to give anybody anything with."

"Anything within reason," Buzz said.

Edwina held up her hand at him like traffic policeman. "But it's no fun to have things unless you share with those you love."

"I feel the same way," Momma said.

"I'm glad to hear that," said Edwina. "Last year Buzz had Aunt Jenny's house painted inside and out."

"She appreciated it," Momma said. She threw me a quick puzzled look.

"She sure did," Buzz said. "Showed her appreciation by giving Edwina the letter her first husband's great-granddaddy wrote from a Yankee jail right after the Civil War."

"War Between the States," Edwina said.

Momma laughed. "Why'd she think Edwina would want that?"

"Oh, she knew Edwina was just crazy about the Civil War and all that old stuff." Buzz shook his head as though that was one he couldn't figure out.

Edwina said, "Poppa," as though reminding him of something.

After a pained glance at Edwina, Buzz said, "If you want some money, Clara, all you have to do is say."

Momma straightened. "You don't find me in want, Buzz."

"Edwina figured you living here with Jean and Lloyd you might like a little cash money of your own."

Momma's lips rolled into a tight line and her eyes flared. "I have plenty of cash money of my own," she said. "I live here for company, not for charity."

Buzz looked embarrassed. "I told that girl...."

Edwina held her hand in his face. "I knew you wouldn't accept money outright, Aunt Clara." She gave Buzz a little nod.

Buzz turned red in the face and then pounded his cane so hard I was afraid he'd gouge a hole in my rug. He said, "I'll give you a thousand dollars for the ladle."

Momma looked as though a handful of firecrackers had exploded inside her head. I jumped up. "Heaven's sake, I've forgotten my manners. Let me get you another piece of cake, Buzz. And I have plenty of unsweetened ice tea, Edwina."

And I was up and passing cake and pouring tea before anyone could speak. By then Momma's face had settled down to near normal, and she smiled and said to Buzz, "Now, tell me about your grandbabies—although I guess they're grandadults by now."

When Buzz started to answer, Edwina jumped in and said, "His grandchildren are fine." That seemed all she had to say about them, but then another thought seemed to strike, and she gave Momma a big smile. "My son Rodney's wife is about to have a new baby, so there'll be yet another to carry on the B for Butterfield."

Momma just looked at her.

"A thousand dollars is lots more than it's worth," Buzz said, "but the girl's got her heart set on adding it to her collection."

"What collection?" I asked, just to be polite.

"I collect family memorabilia from the War Between the States."

Momma shook her head. "Whose family? Didn't your people have ladles of their own to save from the Yankees?"

"Now, Clara," Buzz said, shaking his jowls to quiet Momma. Edwina is from Jasper and folks in that part of Alabama didn't even secede, as Momma knew full well.

Edwina just smiled. "The main point is, we'd do anything to put this squabble aside, and we figured you would, too."

"I have never liked to squabble with Buzz," Momma said.

Buzz bellowed a laugh. "You've done it mighty well not to like it."

"Just hush, Poppa," Edwina said. "Don't you think a thousand dollars is a pretty good price for an old ladle?"

"Not if you can't buy it for that," Momma said.

Buzz ground the rug. "I knew she wouldn't do it."

"Fifteen hundred?" Edwina said.

"Now, Edwina, I told you I wouldn't pay a penny more than a thousand." He tried to stand up, but he couldn't quite make it with so little advance notice.

Edwina gave him a look sharp enough to draw blood. "And I told you I was going to have that ladle no matter what it cost."

"And I told you it was not for sale," Momma said.

Edwina smiled. "We'll go two thousand."

"Just two thousand for an antique like this with a B on it?" Momma said.

"All right then: three thousand." Edwina took a check book from her purse and stuck it under Buzz's nose. "Write the check for three thousand dollars."

"The ladle is not for sale," Momma said.

"Momma chose it for Thad," I said, trying to smooth things over. "B for Blaine."

"I certainly did not," Momma said. "Blaines didn't even come to Alabama until 1897. The B is for Butterfield. Thad wouldn't cheat on something like that, though some might."

Edwina's eyelid flickered, but that was all she showed.

"How much will you take?" she asked.

"Not four, not five, not ten. The ladle is not for sale." Momma smiled her lips. "Now let's not talk about it any more, else we'll end up in another squabble."

Edwina's face clenched into a fist. She said, "This one isn't over yet." That hit the room like a thunderclap.

Buzz put his fingers to his lips and then slumped back into the wing chair. "Clara," he said in a whispery voice. He looked like a balloon losing air.

I turned to watch Momma watching Buzz. The gleam went out of her eyes, and she lifted her hand as though to help Buzz. She seemed paralyzed like that for a good minute. There was not a sound in the room. Then she let her hand drop on Buzz's knee. She said, "I'll give you the ladle, Buzz. For free."

She went straight to the top drawer of the dining room sideboard and took out a brown sack. I was surprised it was there because when we had brought the ladle home, Momma asked me to put it in my silver chest hidden in the den closet. Without a word, she tossed the sack into Edwina's lap. Edwina unzipped it and took out the ladle. If she'd been a rooster, she would have been crowing from the dome of the Alabama state capitol building.

"My goodness, Jean," Momma said, "they've come all this way and you aren't going to show them Lloyd's roses?"

Before I could get to my feet, Edwina was on hers, still grinning. She said, "We better get on the road if we want to beat the heavy traffic going to Birmingham." She looked at the chocolate cake. "Maybe Poppa would like a piece or two of that delicious cake to eat on the ride home. And maybe a little of that nice cheese." She smiled as though she was the kindest person in the world.

Momma looked at Buzz's big paunch, and it was all she could do to hold her tongue but she managed. I wrapped up a couple of pieces of cake and some cheese and crackers, and gave them to Edwina. Buzz hunched forward and, braced on the cane and the arm of the chair, heaved himself up.

We went back down the walk the way we had come up it, Momma leading, me following, them staggering between. Buzz lifted his foot inside the car, and Edwina leaned her shoulder against his rump and shoved. Then she got in the driver's seat.

Momma stuck her head in the car, and she and Buzz gave each other a kiss. As the car jerked away from the curb, Momma called, "Telephone the minute you get home so I'll know you're safe."

When we got back inside, Momma sat down in the very chair Buzz had sat in. "I chose the ladle just to spite Edwina. I was always going to give it to Buzz once we made up." She thought for a while and then shook her head. "I'd rather have chewed a pound of two-penny nails than given in to her, but suppose Buzz had died and us not friends. If that had happened, I'd never have forgiven myself or him."

I said, "You and Buzz could have stopped the squabble any time either of you had wanted to."

She flounced her shoulder at me. "I can't expect you to understand. You and Thad were never like me and Buzz."

I had to admit that was the truth, and I was surprised at how sad that made me.

Mosquitoes

EVERY year we give a Labor Day picnic so Lloyd can say a personal thanks to the twenty-three employees of his tent factory and also provide some fun for them and their families. I've always enjoyed the party though Momma says it is funny how the husband is the host but the wife does the work.

We always hang Japanese lanterns out in the backyard and put citronella candles inside them, to shoo away the mosquitoes. We chill the cold drinks in a big zinc tub, and we always have a keg of ice cold beer.

Everybody says the highlight of the picnic is roasting a pig. I'm not too happy about that little shoat. As the fat begins to melt and fall on the hot coals, I think the first hissing sound is a little squeal and that the little pig-eyes cringe. But Lloyd will not hear of not having one, everybody enjoys it so.

When the pig is nearly done, I stick two or three chickens on the spit—Sylvia the bookkeeper is Jewish, and we don't force her to go public with her diet. She has been at the plant seven years and she always eats the chicken, though I still don't know if she would eat the pig if we didn't also have the chicken. Momma says Sylvia, who is a little plump, would eat anything put before her.

But eating the pig and the chicken and the salad and my special noodles with cottage cheese comes later. First is the fun. There's a city park across the street from our house, and Lloyd sets up horseshoes and three-legged sack races and some plain old races and jumps for the children. And he organizes a softball game for the men and two or three of the younger ladies. Momma says the ladies are just flirting with the men, but some of them are leaner and stronger than some of the puny men with that soft roll of belly under their belt. What I had come to think of as My Problem was the leanest and strongest of all the women who ever worked for Lloyd, even those out in the plant handling the big rolls of plastic.

Alicia—for that was her name—arrived an hour late, after the softball game had started. Lloyd had not joined the game, though he loves to play. He just stayed close to the front door and every minute or two went out on the front porch and with his eyes searched up and down the street. When she finally came, he gave out a big cackle of laughter, as if the world had suddenly got very funny in a good, happy way.

"Come on in, you. I was about to give up on you." He reached out and grabbed her hand and pulled her inside the house. When he saw me at the end of the hall leading to the kitchen, he cried, "Look, Jean, Alicia's here."

I couldn't help thinking a few thoughts. One was that there was no way I could share his pleasure and another was that I hoped no one else had heard him. Unfortunately someone else had. Momma.

"Lloyd, you better go buy some more citronella," she said. "The mosquitoes will have an eating contest on that child's bare legs once dusk sets in."

She pointed at Alicia's long legs, bare from the little piece of cloth across her crotch all the way to her pink-tipped toes. Lloyd's eyes followed Momma's pointing but he managed to mutter, "It's Labor Day. Won't the stores be closed?"

Alicia said, "Mosquitoes don't bite me." She gave Momma a tiny lip-curl. I couldn't exactly blame her but I hate it when young people look at old people that way. I wanted to say, If you behave yourself and are real careful and lucky you may manage to get old, too.

Momma said, "If Jean sat outside in pants like that, the mosquitoes would chew right to the bone."

Lloyd laughed and said, "Once in Pensacola she got bit so bad she looked as if she had poison oak all over her body."

I smiled to show I didn't mind. "I fooled them this time. I took two tablets of Vitamin B."

Alicia said, "Where is everybody?" and looked around as if she was surprised not to see folks lined up along the wall.

"Playing ball. Let's go," Lloyd said. He reached over and took hold of her upper arm and then dropped it quick, as though it was too hot to handle. I could see the color rise up his neck. Then he straightened his shoulders and took her arm again, this time the elbow. "We'll start a new game and you'll play second base on my team," he said, and led her back out the front door to the park.

Momma and I stood at the door and watched them cross the street. "I hope his hand doesn't get grafted onto that arm," Momma said.

I said, "I better see to the noodles. One thing you don't want them is soggy."

At dusk, all the games had been won or lost and almost all the beer had been drunk, and it was time to eat. Every year Momma says we shouldn't serve alcohol with children present, and every year Lloyd answers that the only TV show that doesn't advertise beer is *Sesame Street* so the children already know about it and anyway he wouldn't ask his people to give up a holiday evening if it wasn't going to be fun. Momma primps her mouth and says, I suppose you can't have fun if you don't drink, and Lloyd says Not as much, but he winks at me because he is himself not much of a drinker. If we have company and it is a hot day, we will serve beer, and that is about it.

But if you are not much of a drinker, then a little goes a long way. Lloyd's little had taken a toll. I don't mean he was drunk, but he had become careless and show-offy. When the pig wouldn't easily come off the spit using the forks, he grabbed one side with his hand. I was coming down the kitchen steps with the noodles when I saw him jumping up and down, flapping his hand. Before I could get to him, Alicia stuffed his fingers in the big plastic glass of beer she was holding. I figured that beer wasn't nearly cold enough to do any good, so I grabbed up a cup of ice from the drink tub and ran to him.

He held up his other hand at me as if he were stopping traffic. "I'm all right, I'm being taken care of good," he said. I took a quick look at his hand and saw it wasn't really burned, so I turned away. He called after me, "But I can't carve. Get Gary to do it."

Gary has been plant foreman for a year and a half, ever since he got out of the Marines, and Lloyd says he can do anything. He is somewhere in his thirties, a burly-bodied fellow with hair as yellow as corn, teeth white and big, and eyes the color of a Siamese cat's. I called him and he came rushing over. He slapped the knife across the sharpening steel until the sparks flew. Then he waved the knife around as though it were a sword. "Bruce Lee has been resurrected," he shouted, and everybody laughed. Within a minute that pig was dismembered.

By then Lloyd and Alicia had walked off to the little bench under the magnolia at the corner of the property, Lloyd's hand still in the glass and this time Alicia holding *him* by the arm, as if he couldn't walk it alone. There were two or three people standing nearby, but they came back toward the pig when Lloyd and Alicia sat down.

When Momma and I went to the kitchen, she said, "Is that little thing in Lloyd's office?"

I knew but I said, "What little thing? The stapler?"

Momma primped her lips. "Now, Jean, you know very well what I mean. That girl. Is she out in the plant or in Lloyd's office where he sees her every day?"

I said, "Office, along with Sylvia and Tiny Armstrong."

Momma said, "That girl is common," which, this side of saying someone is immoral, is the worst thing she can say. "And, honey, she spells trouble."

I laughed and said, "Oh, I don't know about that."

But I did know. I had known it from the day Lloyd hired her to answer the phone and pass on to Tiny the orders for the pup tents and the toaster covers. I knew she lived alone and that her brother was in jail. I knew she had gone to the local high school and had taken the business course. I knew she liked to bowl and wanted Lloyd to sponsor a bowling team. Even when he wasn't telling me directly about her, he let her name creep into our evening talk.

I knew all right. But nobody else needed to know I knew. Not Lloyd, not Alicia, not Momma. That way, I figured, maybe the trouble would stay little.

It was nearly dark when I went back outside to make sure everyone was fed. I looked down toward the bench under the magnolia. The Japanese lantern was right above them and I could see the look on Lloyd's face, a look I hadn't seen in a long time. He was leaning down toward Alicia, his lips kind of swollen-looking, his eyes gleaming, his body tight and ready. It was as though he and Alicia were inside a bubble and no one else was present. I thought, My God, he's going to kiss her in front of everybody.

"Lloyd!" I shrieked. When the people turned to look at me, I shouted, "I'll bring you a plate." I snatched Momma's plate of food right out of her hands and ran to the end of the yard.

Lloyd took mighty good care of himself the next couple of weeks. He spent a half hour showering and shaving and drenching himself in aftershave. When he came down to breakfast, his hair was plastered to his scalp, and as the strands dried you could almost hear them snap back to normal. After work he didn't seem as tired as usual, and we made love more often during those weeks, and more energetically than in a long time.

When I compare the two of us, I can hardly blame Lloyd. Just think about it. I am Jean and she is Alicia. I am big and fair and freckled and chewed by mosquitoes, and she is small and dark and smooth and nothing would hurt that lovely flesh. I lumber and she glides. I am forty-nine and his wife for going on twenty-nine years, and she is not yet thirty and unknown.

I understand. I often see young men jogging on the streets, wearing nothing but a skimpy pair of silky shorts, their legs going like pistons, their bodies sweaty, the color of damp gold. I sometimes follow for a block or two. But one big difference is I don't see the same ones every day.

About five weeks after the picnic, Lloyd asked me to invite Alicia over for dinner. We were in bed and it was dark, so I knew he couldn't see that I wasn't a bit surprised. He began to explain.

"She doesn't have any family, honey," he said. "Just a sister in Decatur and that brother locked up in Speigner. Lives in a dinky little apartment in one of those fire traps near Maxwell."

I said, "Have you seen it?"

He said, "Remember couple weeks ago, during Hurricane Jack? That hard rain? I took Alicia home after work." He paused. "And another time or two because she was, you know, not feeling well." He suddenly said, "You don't mind, do you? Me giving Alicia a ride home every now and then?"

"As long as it doesn't make you late for dinner," I said, though I had noticed that for the past week he had been about fifteen minutes behind his usual schedule.

He said, "I thought maybe being around a family might help her settle down."

"Does she need settling? Is she wild?"

"Of course not," he said. "I don't mean settling that way. I mean, like a good example for the future. You know, a nice family?"

"Well, sure," I said. "You want to make it a party? Invite

Tiny Armstrong? Tiny's not married, is he? Maybe him and Alicia?"

I could hear Lloyd blow air through his closed lips to show his scorn. "That sissy? Alicia hardly speaks to him in the office. I don't mean she's cruel or anything, but Tiny just isn't up to her."

"Well," I said. "I'll invite Gary—he's up to most anything."

Lloyd was silent a minute. "I thought it would be just family."

I said, "It can't be just family if Alicia's here, can it? They all know each other, don't they?"

"Yeah, but not well," Lloyd said. "Anyway Gary dud'n work in the office. I don't like mixing the office and the plant."

I thought, He's pretty far gone. I said, "Alicia might like having an eligible man here, mightn't she?"

"Tiny's eligible," Lloyd said. "And I think he kind of likes Alicia. Been making up to her. Gary's too crude. I mean, he's okay for men, but I don't think Alicia likes him."

"I'll invite them both. Gary can be Momma's date. She can handle him. And Tiny can be Alicia's even if he isn't up to her." There wasn't a thing he could say about that.

Lloyd isn't a bit rich or powerful or famous. All he had to offer was his admiration and desire. But that is usually enough to keep the game going when a young woman doesn't have much else to think about. I had sure liked being admired back when I was. I worked at a big Birmingham law firm and the old codgers almost always asked for me out of the secretary pool, and when I walked into their offices to take dictation, I narrowed my eyes a little and glanced through my lashes at them, and I could almost hear their hearts quicken. And, unlike Alicia, I wasn't that much of a looker. Just young and full of energy. I wasn't worried about Alicia in any final way—I just wanted to get through it without too much pain for me and Lloyd.

❧

The night we had the dinner party, I thought Lloyd would stay at the plant until the usual time, but he came home an hour early. He shaved for the second time that day and took a shower and put on fresh clothes, including a necktie which he almost never wears. When he came down the stairs, he smiled at me. I almost expected him to say, "How do I look, Mom?" just like my son Carl does when he's home.

"I'll go get Alicia," he said.

"Tiny isn't going to pick her up?"

Lloyd looked right at me without batting an eye. "He doesn't know where she lives."

Before Lloyd got back, Tiny arrived. He is the only tiny person called Tiny that I ever saw. Although he is normal height, all his appendages are small, shoulders, hands, feet, ears. His features are so tiny you could have covered his whole face with a tea cup. You wouldn't think he could do very much, but Lloyd says Tiny has never in the twelve years he has run the order department made a mistake. Momma says God made such a big mistake to begin with there wasn't enough left to make even a small one out of.

The next to come was Gary, looking just as I knew he would, busting with energy, gleaming with the pleasure he took in life.

The next was Momma, though she only came from her room down the hall. She shook hands first with Tiny and then with Gary. Gary kept hold of her hand and kind of twirled her toward the sofa where he sat. Even after she sat down, he still held her hand.

"I'mo tell your fortune," he said. He began to trace the lines of her palm with his fingertips but before he could finish the lifeline Momma had jerked away.

She said, "I don't believe in that stuff."

"I don't either," Gary said. "It was just a pretext to hold your hand, Mrs. Blaine."

Momma laughed. "That's just what I don't believe in. I'm too old."

Gary said. "Let's just test that proposition." He reached over for her hand again, but Momma wouldn't let him take it. The two of them began a little game of hand-snatching, both of them laughing. If I ever saw a man who knew his power, it was Gary. I could feel a little tremor in myself, seeing the way he was playing with Momma. Tiny just watched, though he clutched his hands between his knees so tight that his thumb knuckles whitened.

Lloyd and Alicia were a good half-hour late. Alicia had on a fuzzy purple sweater so tight you could see her bra lines. Her breasts were high on her chest and pointed. When I was in high school there was a girl with breasts like that, and the boys called her Six Shooters. The girls called her fast. At the sight of Alicia, Tiny turned crimson and ducked his head, but Gary jumped up.

"Worth the wait," he shouted. "You beautiful sexy thing." He stretched forth his arms as if he was going to tackle her.

Alicia laughed and said, "Down, boy." But she gave him a look that would have told a poodle dog to keep jumping.

Then Gary made a heavy dog-breathing sound, his tongue lolling out of his mouth. He said, "Want me to roll over on my back?"

Alicia said, "If you do, maybe I'll scratch your belly."

Lloyd looked as if he wanted to do something but he didn't know what. Momma said, "Speaking of dogs, we once had a blind mutt dog that Poppa trained to collect the eggs from the chickens."

"You're fibbing, Mrs. Blaine," Gary said. "You're making it up." He winked at Alicia.

"It's the truth," Momma said. "That dog would use his nose to raise up the hen and his long old tongue to lift out the egg." And she was off with one of her crazy farm stories. I never knew whether they were true—I just knew that when a situation needed one, she had one.

I put Alicia between Gary and Lloyd, with Momma across the table next to Tiny. Momma and Gary did most of the talking. Momma told some more farm stories and then Gary told a story about being in the Marines.

For the first time that evening, Tiny volunteered to talk. He said, in his slow quiet voice, "I was in the army." He shot Alicia a look, but she didn't return it.

"Goodness," Lloyd said, "you were in the army? I didn't know that, Tiny. You never told me that." Lloyd showed such interest you would have thought Tiny had been hiding the Congressional Medal of Honor.

"Not during a war, though," Tiny said. He looked around as though he was horrified at taking up so much space in the conversation.

Momma said. "It wasn't your fault there wasn't a war."

Tiny looked ashamed. "I was glad."

"Why'd you join the army?" Lloyd asked as if he really wanted to know.

"He wanted to serve his country," Momma said. "Didn't you, Tiny?"

"No'm," Tiny said, staring at the tips of his little fingers as if something helpful might be written there. He looked up at Alicia. "I wanted to get away from my mother."

We all laughed, because we knew he lived with his mother. Even Tiny laughed. He sighed and said, "I had my four years' freedom, I was ready to come back and settle down."

Lloyd said, "I didn't know I had another old serviceman working at the plant. You knew I was in the army, didn't you? Right at the start of Vietnam."

"You were shot at, weren't you?" Alicia said.

If ever a man looked as though he wanted to tell a lie, it was Lloyd then. He looked at me and he looked at Momma and I heard him wishing we weren't there. He said, "I wasn't actually in Nam. I was stationed in Okinawa. But it was during. I could have been sent to the front. I'da been glad to go, too."

"Huf," Alicia said, shrugging. "I thought you told me you were really in a war."

Gary said, "I was in Iraq, right in the thick of it." He smirked at Alicia and started rolling up the sleeve of his blue silk shirt. "I got this in Cyprus on the way back from Saudi." It was a big moon face topped by a little military cap.

"Looks like Stormin' Norman, dud'n it?" Gary said. "Watch him grin." Gary flexed his muscle and the mouth spread wide.

Momma said, "Well, he's got a lot to be pleased about."

Gary said, "That's the way, id'n it? The privates get killed and the generals don't do anything and make ten million dollars."

"He won the war is all," Lloyd said, "and you didn't get killed."

"Wud'n him who won it and I was a sergeant," Gary answered. He turned to look at Alicia, who was drinking her ice tea. His eyes gleamed. "But thank God my privates wud'n killed either."

Alicia choked and spurted a few drops of tea onto her plate and put her napkin up to her mouth.

Lloyd said, "I don't think boys getting killed is funny."

I got up. "Anybody, any more lamb? Potatoes? Broccoli?" I went to the kitchen door to show I was willing to bring out more food. From where I was I had an angle to see under the table, and I saw Gary's foot move over to cover Alicia's and I knew his knee was resting against hers.

"Your privates dying ain't a bit funny, boss," Gary said. "But I can attest that mine did'n."

"I bet they were eager to go home, though," Alicia said.

"Stop it," Lloyd shouted. He stood up so fast I thought his chair would go over behind him. We all looked at him. He stood there wringing his napkin, crimson in the face, staring down the table at Alicia.

I said, "Lloyd, honey."

And Gary said, "Yessir, General," and brought his hand to his brow in a quick salute and bobbed his head.

Lloyd looked from Alicia to Gary and then back. He said. "What I meant was…" but he could not think of anything he could have meant other than what he did: whatever you are doing to each other, stop it. He sat back down.

And then there was Momma again, smoothing an awkward situation. "Jean, are we going to have dessert? I guess you forgot that lemon chiffon pie you spent half the afternoon making. Honestly, Tiny, I'm not the only one getting senile around here. Speaking of which, I had this crazy old aunt who lost her mind. Her children were going to put her in a home, but she fooled them. She sold her farmhouse without telling them and put the money in the stock market and tripled it before they could get a court order to take it away from her."

I went into the kitchen and cut the pie into eight pieces instead of six so I could offer seconds to Gary and Tiny. When I carried the tray to the dining room, Momma and Gary were going at each other about who was the biggest liar. Tiny looked kind of tense and alert, as though he had money on the winner, and Alicia laughed at almost every word, in that excited way young women like Alicia have when there's a man like Gary around. Lloyd looked as doleful as an old dog.

When we all got to the front door after dinner, Lloyd opened the coat closet and took down his hat.

I said, "Honey, maybe Tiny could drop Alicia off?"

"I be glad to do it," Tiny said, his eyes brightening, "even though it's a little out of the way."

Gary said, "Don't worry about it, I'm taking her. It's all already arranged." He looked at Alicia and winked.

Lloyd stood in the middle of the front hall, twirling his hat on his hand, looking at it so intently you would have thought he was practicing a difficult trick. Then he looked up and said, "Thanks, Gary. I'm a little tired tonight."

I could feel myself grinning all over, my knees, my elbows, my scalp. Momma said, "It was so nice to have you folks here. Come again real soon."

And they all said they would.

As the three of them walked down the walk, Momma said, "You have such nice young people working for you, Lloyd." Lloyd and I stood at the door and watched Gary throw his arm across Alicia's shoulders and draw her to him. Their laughter floated back to us.

"Yes'm," Lloyd said.

I told Momma and Lloyd to just go on to bed. I put the dishes and glasses into the machine, and I filled the sink with soapy water to soak the pots and pans, and then I went upstairs. I thought maybe Lloyd would be asleep, but he wasn't. The light was still on and he was lying on his back in bed, his hands locked behind his head. I went to the closet and took off my dress. Somehow I have never liked removing all my clothes in front of him, though I don't mind being without any on at all. I slipped on my nightgown and went to sit at the vanity to take off my face.

"Peas in a pod, aren't they?" I said. Lloyd groaned agreement. "Tiny's too nice for a woman like that. He's well out of it."

He said, "He's not the one was in it." He reared up on his elbows to catch my eye in the mirror, and I frowned and primped my lips at him.

I said, "Let's don't rehash tonight. I'm too tired."

He fell back and turned on his side and buried his face in his pillow. "Oh, Jean," he said in a hollow, mournful voice as though he was at the very bottom of a deep well. I don't believe I've ever felt sorrier for anyone. When I had wiped off the cream from my face, I turned out the light and got in bed beside him, and I hugged him tight.

What's Right for Jenny

JENNY had been a late arrival in the Butterfield family, eleven years younger than Momma and as different from her as Crackerjacks from corn-on-the-cob. Momma said Jenny was always a step slower than the rest of the family but made up for it by being the prettiest and the sweetest. She is still pretty and sweet, though Momma likes to point out that she totes fifty pounds too much of that nice pink flesh.

By the time Jenny was born, Granma was tired of chasing children and left her upbringing to Momma. Momma looked after Jenny as close as she could, but one day she must have blinked and Jenny at sixteen ran off with a boy named Skippy Doyle. Right at the end of the Korean War, Skippy was loading cargo on the Mobile dock when the rope slipped and squshed him. Back Jenny came to Momma.

By the time my recollections are clear, Jenny had slipped away again, to Sylacauga with Horace. Horace sold beauty supplies all over North Alabama and eight years later he ran off to Reno with a beauty parlor operator from Opelika.

Nearly four years of widowhood, grass or real, were enough for Jenny, even with hanky panky in between, and so without even telling Momma, she married Jimmy. He was the projectionist at the Sylacauga picture show, and we got free tickets whenever we visited. But too much squinting at the silver screen had dimmed his eyesight, and one day he stepped off the curb against the light, and a Mayflower van struck him dead.

"Some folks aren't meant to be married," Momma told Jenny. "You not having children and with what Mayflower paid you, you don't need a husband. And, my goodness, you're coming up fifty years old."

Jenny cried and said, "But I can't live without love."

Momma was truly disgusted after Jenny married JoTom. She said all JoTom wanted out of life was to sink his teeth in hard-fried chicken and rest his bottom on a soft cushion. She said he married for money and since Jenny had so little it showed what a puny fellow he was. He was ten years younger than Jenny, duck-legged and pie-faced. They were mighty romantic, though, holding hands and stealing pinches. Even Momma had to admit that for over ten years JoTom made Jenny happy. Not that that was hard to do: she had been happy with Horace right up to reading the signature at the bottom of the postcard from Nevada.

When JoTom died of heart failure, Lloyd and I drove Momma up from Montgomery for the funeral. "Nobody can accuse me of hypocrisy," she said, "so I won't even pretend to grieve. Jenny has the worst taste in men I ever saw. They all die."

JoTom's funeral took place in a ramshackle Baptist church, stuck between a subdivision of little houses and an alfalfa field. It had spent its life as a country church but it had aspirations. In the tiny vestibule was a drawing six feet long and a yard high of the church the congregation planned to build. That church looked to be about the size of the Alabama state capitol and had two-story columns all around. Across the top was a big sign in fancy gilt letters: "We build to build Christians for the Greater Glory of God."

On one side of the drawing was something called "The Roll of Honor." It had people's names listed under titles like "Patron Over $5000," "Contributor $1000-4999," and on down to "Friend up to $50" with one name and two Anonymouses.

"I don't see JoTom's name," Lloyd said, looking at the lists.

"Is there a group called Deadbeat?" Momma asked, glinting her eyes.

Just as we were chuckling, a very large lady entered the vestibule and glowered at us. She had on a big flowered tent-like dress, one of those that aren't supposed to touch the body anywhere but the shoulders so nobody knows what's inside. She carried a purse with a long strap over her forearm and her forearm rested on her stomach. As she walked, the purse banged between her knees. Her expression said the church was her personal property and we better watch out.

Momma can win over anybody when she sets her mind to it, and I could see her working up a sweet, grieving expression. She went right up to the lady and speaking in that hushed tone people use at funerals began to say how sad it was about JoTom. When she found out the lady was the preacher's wife, not JoTom's kin, Momma changed to a smile and congratulated her on the new church. The lady pointed out which wing was the sanctuary and which was the gym and where the Ladies Auxiliary and the AA would meet. Momma made herself look envious, and the lady swelled up so proud that I thought she would bust the seams of that big dress.

About then Jenny drove up with Uncle Buzz and his son, Burt Junior, and Burt's wife, Edwina, in Buzz's Cadillac car. As the oldest living Butterfield male, Buzz took the lead on family occasions like funerals, although he was so flabby and weak I wondered if he'd have a stroke before he could hoist his body out of the car.

Poor Jenny. She could hardly make it up the steps even with Edwina lifting her on one side and Burt Junior on the other. As soon as they got through the door, the preacher rushed up the aisle and shoved Burt Junior aside and took Jenny's elbow. The preacher's name was Frank Collard. He was lanky and swarthy and had a knotty sad face. I thought in his black suit he looked like Abraham Lincoln.

I don't think Jenny heard a word of the service. She spent the entire time swaying and wailing. But Reverend Collard went right on talking, mostly about how faithful and loving Jenny had been but occasionally remembering to say something nice about JoTom. When he finished, he invited everybody to come up to take a final look before the coffin was closed. Jenny was last, of course, and she gave out a howl and collapsed over the coffin as if her bones had thawed into slush.

Momma whispered, "You'd think she'd be used to losing husbands by now." Momma hates it when people take advantage of an opportunity to give in like that.

The reverend and Burt each took an elbow and with each step lifted Jenny up and forward, bouncing her back up the aisle.

I drove Momma to Sylacauga every other Friday to take Jenny out to lunch at the motel cafe and otherwise lift her spirits, and every other Friday it was the same thing: Jenny was crying when we got there and crying when we left. She had cried so much her skin looked as though a tropical disease had taken root and her eyes were so swollen she had completely lost the whites. She said widowhood just got harder, not easier, because when the last one left she had to grieve all over again for the others, even Horace. Her sorrow had kept on accumulating, and by the time she got to JoTom her heart had busted wide open.

And every Friday Momma told her how to run the rest of her life.

"Don't feel so sorry for yourself," Momma finally said. "You've got your house, you've got your health, and you've got enough money."

"But I haven't got anybody to love," Jenny said, sniffling.

"Surely you've had your fill of that. Find some other interest."

Jenny sniffled again. "What else is there besides love?"

"Crossword puzzles," Momma said, flapping her hand in disgust. That made Jenny cry all the harder. Momma patted her shoulder and said, "All right now, I was just teasing. I know you never could do crossword puzzles. But what about ladies' clubs? Or how about that fancy new church? You always were religious."

Momma and Jenny and the other Butterfields were brought up to be religious. Granma was real strict. The children had to go to church on Sundays and to attend any revival in the vicinity of Demopolis. Whenever the preacher was to visit, Granma hid the bicycle cards in her apron pocket so nobody would get caught playing.

Momma raised me and Thad to be churchgoers. She claimed that though people who went to church might not be good deep down, they wanted their neighbors to think they were, and so they behaved themselves better than average. But she wasn't as strict as Granma. With so many tent revivals in a big city like Birmingham, she figured people at one revival would think we were at another so we never went to any.

"That's not hypocritical, is it, Mrs. Blaine?" Lloyd asked.

That hurt Momma so bad it was all I could do to keep her from going into a pout that might have lasted a week.

A few weeks after Momma told Jenny to get interested in the church, when we went for our usual visit, we saw a broken-down old car at the curb. It was Reverend Collard's and he was inside talking with Jenny, and Jenny wasn't crying. Momma gave me a See-how-right-I-was look.

"Don't let us interrupt," she said. "We'll just listen. Jean, be quiet, now." She flapped her hand at me and sat down on the edge of the sofa and nodded at the reverend to go on.

The reverend straightened back his shoulders and cleared his throat. "I been telling Miss Jenny that like the Bible says, God moves in a mysterious way, His wonders to perform."

He paused and shot a look at Momma. Then he lifted his arm and pointed his index finger at the overhead light in the ceiling. "I been telling her God chasteneth whom he loveth." He paused again and let his arm drop. I could tell he was trying to crank up, but the spirit just wouldn't move him. "Well, that's what I been telling her," he finished.

"That's just the thing Jenny needs to hear," Momma said, smiling encouragement at him. "Say some more."

Reverend Collard looked desperate and then jumped up. "I wish I could stay," he said, "but others need me, too."

He went over to Jenny and put his hands on her shoulders. I felt Momma lean forward and tighten up. Reverend Collard said, "I'll be back tomorrow. You know you can always count on my help, Miss Jenny." He patted her for a minute or two.

Momma gave the reverend a look that would have set fire to a mud puddle. "The Bible says the Lord helps those who help themselves," she said.

"I'm trying, Sister," Jenny said. "But I need more help than I can give myself." She glanced up at the reverend and her eyes teared up.

"Isn't that what I'm here for?" Momma almost shouted. "You sit still. I'll see the reverend out."

When Momma came back into the living room, she started right in. "Tall, dark, and unhandsome," she said. "Did you ever see a face looked more like the walking away end of a mangy cat?"

Jenny said, "Now, Sister, people can't be blamed for their looks."

"Maybe they can't help being ugly, but they can stay home," Momma said.

I said, "Next best to home for being ugly must be the church because folks are more forgiving there. Maybe that's why most preachers are so ugly."

Jenny grinned and slapped the air and said, "Y'all." Then she remembered and broke into sobs. "I won't ever be happy again," she said, and Momma began to pat her.

On the way back to Montgomery, Momma asked what I really

thought about the preacher. I said I agreed with her—he was not pretty.

She said, "Now, Jean, I don't care about being ugly. I'm talking about him putting his hands all over Jenny."

"Just to comfort her," I said. "Preachers do that."

"They do a lot more than that."

"Anyway, he's married. That big woman in the flowered dress?"

"Ha!" Momma said. "That never stopped a man yet. Or Jenny either."

I said, "With a wife like that old sow, who could blame him for stealing a pinch or two." We had a good laugh at that, but she would not be deterred. "A preacher gone bad is the worst gone-bad in the world. That fellow's been saving up his devilment for forty years."

I said, "Now Momma, he's just doing what he would for any member of his flock."

"And he'll fleece her for sure," she answered.

"She hasn't got much to fleece," I pointed out.

"I know exactly what she has to fleece," Momma said.

The next Friday Jenny and Reverend Collard were sitting side by side on the sofa when we arrived, their eyes glued to the television set. Jenny put her finger to her lips for us to be quiet. On the screen was a red-headed man wearing a sombrero and a western string tie with a big silver cross holding the ends together. He was talking about Africans and Asians and Eskimos, and as he talked their pictures appeared, looking kind of moth-eaten but cheerful. Written over their faces were the words "Your Prayers and Contributions Will Bring a Billion Souls to God," and an 800 number and the address of the Gospel Broadcasting Company. Then the pictures vanished and the camera came in close on the red-headed man, and a big choir all in white appeared in the background.

Jenny sighed and turned off the TV and gave us our hello-kisses. The reverend said, "We sure enjoy the television ministers, don't we, Miss Jenny? They have the old time religion, don't they, Miss Jenny?"

Momma said, "Those folks will say anything for a dollar."

"Now, Sister," Jenny said, sitting down in a chair next to Momma's, "that man is converting the atheists and the natives."

"That's just so he'll have more poor folks to squeeze money out of," Momma said.

"Now, Sister," Jenny said, "he doesn't ask you to give more than you can."

"Don't come running to me when you get fleeced," Momma said.

"Now, Sister," Jenny said, but she seemed not to be able to think what to say next, and she looked at Reverend Collard for help.

"Sister's right, Miss Jenny," he said, giving Momma a cajoley smile that sure didn't favor Abe Lincoln. "We have to be careful where we put our love and our trust."

"The minute you let down your guard," Momma said, "something nasty will sneak in." She looked as though she was seeing something nasty.

Jenny began to whimper and press her fingertips into her eyeballs. Reverend Collard ran to her, but Momma shot up straight and hipped him out of the way.

"I believe I know best how to take care of Jenny," she said. "I been doing it long enough. Here: I'll show you how to get out."

All during lunch at the motel, Momma warned Jenny against trusting what she called Swaggart and Braggart and Bakker and Faker. I knew she really meant Reverend Collard. Then she plain out and said it.

"Seems to me that preacher fellow comes around a tad too often."

"I thought you told me to find an interest in the church," Jenny said.

Momma put her hands flat on the table and leaned toward Jenny. "The church is stone and wood and brick, Jenny, and the preachers are flesh."

"Now, Sister," Jenny said, "he's been so nice. I don't know what I would have done without him."

"I'm more worried about what you might do *with* him," Momma hissed. "You know your weakness."

Jenny reached into the front of her dress for her handkerchief. "You shouldn't suspect me like that when I'm still grieving for JoTom."

"JoTom was a fine man," Momma said.

When we got there the next Friday, Jenny was alone. She gave Momma a great big smile and said, "Oh, Sister, I'm the happiest woman in the world. He has come into my life." She pressed her hands together on top of her bosom and rocked from side to side.

Momma threw herself into a chair and stared at Jenny.

"I was sitting there crying," Jenny said, pointing at the sofa, "because I thought I would never love again. I saw myself going into the kitchen and pulling up a chair and turning on the oven. You know my oven is gas?"

"Don't you dare," Momma said in a threatening voice, "no matter what you've done."

"So just as I stood up and walked to the kitchen door," Jenny said, her eyes on the ceiling, "I heard a voice."

"You telling me you didn't even know he was in the house?" Momma said.

"He wasn't, before," Jenny said. "But He was sitting in that chair you're sitting in and He said, 'I love you,' plain as anything. And I instantly knew what it was I had been waiting for."

"I could have told you that," Momma said.

Jenny looked at Momma. "I sat back down, and I said, 'I love you, too.' Oh, Sister, this is the truest love of all."

Momma leaned toward her and looked fierce. "Don't you know that knotty-faced man is out to take advantage of you?"

Jenny suddenly looked frightened. "It wasn't Reverend Collard," she said. "It was Jesus."

Momma leaned back. "What are you talking about now?" she said.

"You know Jesus," Jenny said.

"Of course I know Jesus," Momma said, flouncing her shoulder. "But you were talking about that preacher man."

"No, I wasn't. I was talking about Jesus," Jenny said, "Sister, you don't have to worry about that kind of thing any more. I'm saved now."

Momma gave me a look to see what I thought. I didn't think anything yet, and so I just shrugged. She turned back to Jenny. "Are you claiming you've been born again?"

"Oh, Lord God yes," Jenny said. "I'm *saved*." She closed her eyes, reared back her head, and gave out a blissful smile. Then she opened her eyes and looked at Momma. "Aren't you glad for me?" she asked.

Momma frowned. "Well," she said, looking first at Jenny and then at me. And then another, "Well," and then, "Well, isn't it what I told you to do?"

Jenny's face brightened. "You led me there, all right," she said. "If it hadn't been for you, I wouldn't have got born again, would I?" She looked around. "Isn't it time for us to go to the motel for lunch? Y'all don't want to be late driving home."

Momma was unusually quiet during lunch, and I could tell she was thinking hard. When we had eaten their special egg salad sandwich, she frowned and looked right into Jenny's face.

"You're not fibbing me, are you, Jenny? I mean, you are born again?"

Jenny looked wide-eyed. "I never was smart enough to fib you, Sister."

"I don't suppose so," Momma said.

"You won't have to worry about me doing something foolish ever again. "

"I hope that's so, but a lot of born-agains are quick in quick out."

"Some hold," Jenny said. "You ought to try it yourself."

"And some of them get mighty obnoxious telling other people how to do." Momma blew air through her nose to show what she thought of being told how to do.

Jenny looked as though she was tuning up again to cry, so I jumped in and spoke right to Momma. "Some folks tell other people how to do whether they're born again or not." Jenny threw me a smile of appreciation, but Momma didn't get it at all. She just went right on talking.

"I'm in favor of religion," she said. "I believe in God and all, though I've been too busy to be a fanatic myself. But if it keeps you out of trouble, then I'm for it. When's the last time He visited?"

"Yesterday evening," Jenny said, looking wide-eyed at Momma, "but just for a minute."

The waitress came up with the bill and twirled it around above our heads. Momma reached up and grabbed it. "I'm paying. I guess He's making sure of you. Does He come often?"

"Just every once in a while. Just to talk." Jenny said. Her voice had begun to quiver a little. "I'm not encouraging him, Sister. Honest I'm not." Momma was too busy tallying the bill to hear.

"I think Momma is talking about Jesus," I murmured "not Reverend Collard."

The blood rushed into Jenny's face so fast her eyeballs began to glow and pulse. She gave me a pleading look, and I raised my eyebrows and shook my head to tell her I wouldn't say a word.

"That waitress didn't refill our ice tea," Momma said. "Five percent's plenty." Jenny looked at me and smiled.

I stopped the car at the curb in front of Jenny's but kept the motor running while we said goodbye. I wanted to get

Momma out of there as quickly as I could. Jenny said, "I reckon you won't need to come up to check on me so often, will you, Sister?"

Momma nodded. "My job's done, now you've done what I told you and got religion."

"You always have known what was right for me," Jenny said, getting out of the car. She stuck her head through the open window and kissed Momma on the cheek. "And we both thank you. I mean, Jesus and I."

"If you have any bad temptations, you call, hear?" Momma said.

"I will, Sister, but I don't expect any."

As we started away from the curb, Momma said. "Well, I guess she's safe for a while." She had a proud look on her face.

I said, "You'd know it if she weren't, wouldn't you?"

"Oh, yes, I'd know," she said.

I looked in the rearview mirror. A rattletrap car was rounding the corner, and Jenny was dancing toward it, up the sidewalk, her arms swinging, her skirts swirling. She looked like a young woman again, free again, falling in love again.

The New South

MOMMA always despised the words "New South." She took it as a personal affront when people talked about how much better things are now than they were back then when she was growing up. She said praising the new proves you don't understand the old. She said people then were lots more accommodating and pleasant to be around. Nowadays, she said, men had just as soon knock her to the ground to get on a bus first, women smoke in public and eat while walking down the street, children say ma'am as if they're making fun of you, and whites and coloreds are enemies instead of the friends they were in the old days.

When she talked like that, my son, Carl, laughed and called her Miss Scarlett. And then they went at each other. Carl is a great joker, and if there's one thing he enjoys it's riling Momma, and one thing Momma enjoys it's besting him in an argument. Some people say Carl is my pet, but I had enough bad experience with Momma favoring Thad to not have a pet. And anyway if I had shown Carl any partiality, Sara would have held her breath until she fainted, or I did.

In October, when Carl came up from Mobile for the weekend, he wasn't in the house ten minutes before he got the subject going. It was a hot Indian summer day and the four of us were sitting out in the breeze-through drinking ice tea. The autumn reds and oranges reflecting on Carl's face and his white shirt matched his red hair, and his face seemed to glow like fire.

He was telling us about a twelve-story apartment building the construction company he worked for was planning to put up. He had watched the wreckers destroy the rickety old downtown house the building would replace, and he said he had seen a family of rats run up from the basement.

"One of them was so old," he said, "the others carried him out on a little stretcher wrapped in a Confederate flag."

When Lloyd and I finished laughing, Momma primped her lips and said, "You New South folks are destroying our heritage." That was enough to set Carl off teasing her.

He said, "The New South is going to sqush you if you stand in the way of progress, Granny."

Momma looked at him as if he were a nest of vipers. She said, "It is not progress to destroy our lovely old mansions."

I shook my head at Carl, but he winked at me and went right on. "Why, Miss Scarlett, I didn't know your family had a lovely old mansion. I thought you grew up on a broken-down farm with an outhouse."

"I never pretend and you know it, but those fine old ante-bellum homes are part of my heritage, and yours too, if you had sense enough to see it, but you don't," Momma said, flouncing her shoulder at him. "Anyway, we had running water by the time I was seven."

"I hear the whole family had to take a course at the grammar school on how to flush the toilet," Carl said. Even Momma had to laugh at that. Then he said, "Come on out, Loretta."

I looked up and Loretta was standing in the doorway. She has ironed and cleaned for us since Carl was in junior high. Her skin is the color of bark, and she is so tall she almost reaches the top of the doorjamb and so thin standing sideways she hardly casts a shadow. Carl once said to her if she had been a man she could have made three million dollars a year playing basketball instead of five fifty an hour plus carfare.

Carl said, "Granny's been telling us about the first time

she used a flush toilet. I bet you can remember that, too, can't you?"

Momma frowned. "I'm sure Loretta wants to get on with her work," she said, smiling at Loretta to encourage her to leave.

"How about some ice tea?" Lloyd said.

"Ice tea don't quench my thirst none," Loretta said. "It takes Co-Cola. But I'll rest awhile long's all y'all are resting too." She refused the chair Carl offered, but she kind of hooked what little bottom she had on the edge of the railing, so one foot was off the floor, and she leaned back against the post.

Carl said, "I'd like to hear what Loretta has to say about the New South. You for it or agin it?"

I said, "Carl, just stop it."

"Don't worry—I ain't going to answer him," Loretta said. "I know Carl just teasing his gramma. He know how to get under her skin just like a little chigger." Loretta covered her mouth with her bony hand and snuffled a laugh.

"He's not under my skin at all," Momma said. "He's just acting the fool. Sometimes I think he shows a tad too much talent playing that role." She narrowed her eyes and shot me a look to be sure I got the dig.

Loretta stood up and shook her head and snuffled again. "The fire out here getting too hot. I'mo go finish my ironing."

Momma smiled her approval. "Now take special care of my blue voile dress, you hear?" She said this as though she and Loretta were in a conspiracy.

"I ain't ruined one yet," Loretta said.

Momma frowned her forehead but kept her mouth smiling. "I mean, those little scallops at the neck?"

Carl said, "Why don't you go on strike, Loretta?"

Loretta moved off toward the door. "It ain't got to that yet," she said. Then she turned and grinned at Carl.

When Loretta disappeared, into the house, Momma whipped around to face Carl. "I don't appreciate one bit what you just said," she said.

"Loretta going on strike?" Carl said, laughing.

"Y'all," I said, flapping my hand at them. But I could no more stop Momma than I could Carl.

"Fortunately she has too much sense to listen to you," Momma said. "She knows her place."

Carl poufed air through his lips and said, "I guess her place is standing over an ironing board."

Lloyd and I looked at each other. Lloyd said, "Now, you know your gramma didn't mean that. She meant..." He raised his hand as though releasing into the air whatever it was he thought she did mean.

Momma looked peeved for a minute, then smiled a secret smile. She leaned forward and with an innocent, wide-eyed look said, "I suppose you iron your own shirts, Carl?"

Carl laughed and said, "Of course I don't. I take them to the laundry."

Momma leaned back, still looking innocent, and I knew she was up to something. "And I suppose the women at the laundry are treated lots better than your mother and I treat Loretta," she said. "I understand they get to sit down and watch the television while they iron, the way Loretta does, and the Co-Cola is on the house the way it is here. And they borrow money when they need it and pay it back when they get good and ready. And I bet they appreciate it when you go in and thank them for doing your ironing." She quickly cut me and Lloyd a triumphant glare.

"They get paid for the ironing they do," Carl said. He was still smiling, but I knew he was stung.

Momma leaned back in triumph. "If I had to iron—and I've done my share I'll tell you—I'd a heap rather do it in this nice cool house than at some steaming laundry. Maybe you should try ironing your own shirts, Carl, so you'd know a little more what you're talking about."

Carl flung up his arms. "Granny, the point is, working at the laundry isn't personal the way working for some individual is."

"I guess that makes it better, people not caring about you." Momma lowered her eyelids and cut a look at me.

Carl tried to pretend he was amused, but he was smarting. He said, "Can't you see the difference between you doing something nice for somebody out of the kindness of your heart and the person getting it because it's their right?"

"Kindness gives me more pleasure than any right ever could."

"Especially if you have the power," Carl said. "But suppose you had to rely on somebody else's kindness?"

"I hope they'd be as nice as I am."

Carl threw his hands in the air, pretending to be only pretending he had lost the argument, and Momma smirked, pretending she was sure she had won.

When I went into the kitchen to pay Loretta late that afternoon, I found Momma admiring the way her voile dress had been ironed. "You are mighty smart with that iron," she said, examining the scalloped neckline and then the hem.

"You ain't apt to forget how to do it when you do it all the time," Loretta said.

"I just wanted to thank you," Momma said. "Lot of younguns take things for granted, but us old folks know how to appreciate."

"Old folks don't have much to appreciate. Might as well take advantage when you get the chance," Loretta said. As she stood up, she reminded me of one of those old-timey fold-up yardsticks you straighten out section by section.

Momma shook her head impatiently. It was clear she wasn't getting what she wanted. "Anything you want or need?" she asked Loretta.

"I ain't got time to make that long a list," Loretta said. She snuffled a laugh. "Too bad Carl don't live here."

Momma frowned and looked disconcerted. Later, sitting in the den watching television, she said, "What's gotten into Loretta?"

∾

Carl wasn't due to come home again until Thanksgiving Day. By then the weather had turned cold. We'd even had a flake or two of snow. It's funny to me what people think the weather in Alabama is. A daughter of a cousin who strayed off to Montana came visiting and was shocked to learn we wear sweaters and even overcoats. She said she expected to see everybody in bikinis.

On Wednesday, Loretta brought a rhubarb pie she had made for Carl. It is his very favorite dessert. When Momma saw the pie, she said, "I hope you didn't put any of the stalk in, Loretta. You know it's poisonous."

Momma didn't see Loretta roll her eyeballs, but if she had been listening she could have heard them whirring.

"No'm," Loretta said, "I decided not to since Carl's going to be eating it."

I laughed to show they were both joking. "Anyway, I'd be safe," I said. I hate rhubarb. When I was little, we had it a lot because Poppa liked it so—that's where Carl inherited his inclination. To me, rhubarb boiled was just pink phlegm, and once Momma quit making me eat it, when I was about nine, I never let it pass my lips. But I didn't want my prejudices to keep Carl from enjoying something he really loves or Loretta from fixing something special for somebody she loves. I say she loves him, but Carl says I can't say what Loretta feels because we don't really know. I guess that's right.

Carl called Wednesday evening to say he wouldn't be able to spend the weekend because the fellow from the New York bank was there and he had to get back to Mobile for a Friday meeting but could he bring the fellow with him for Thanksgiving dinner? Of course I said of course.

I was up early to stuff and cook the twenty-two pound turkey. We sure didn't need one that size just for the five of us, but Lloyd insisted. He said he couldn't get a fair fight with a little bird—he always lost. He couldn't find the joints and ended up twisting off the limbs and slinging pieces of skin and drips of grease halfway across the dining room. The fact is, even with a big one it usually got down to hand-to-hand combat. Yet carve he would. He said it ought to be done in public, and anyway it was the man's part of the holiday ceremony.

Momma came into the kitchen just as I was taking the sweet potatoes out of the oven.

"I thought you said they were coming for dinner," she said.

"It's not one yet, Momma. They aren't due until two-thirty."

Momma said, "They're probably out looking for another beautiful mansion to tear down. Just like Sherman marauding through Georgia." I dumped a potato on to the formica counter and began to pick off the skin with a fork. She said, "I don't see why they have to have a New York bank. I don't suppose Alabama banks are still using Confederate money, are they?"

"No'm," I said.

Just then, Lloyd stuck his head around the corner of the door. "Are they here yet?" he asked.

I set the potato down very carefully so I could turn around to give him a dirty look. "Not unless they're hiding under the bed," I said. "Go sharpen the carving knife on your wheel." And take Momma with you, I wanted to add, but please don't sharpen her.

"Well, hand it to me, will you?" He held his hand out, though the wooden holder was not two yards from him and I would have had to walk across the room. It's funny how when people are doing you a favor they expect you to wait on them while they do it. I turned back to picking at the potato.

Momma said, "It's almost a sin for Carl to bring a stranger for Thanksgiving."

"I guess the man didn't have any place else to go," I said.

"Is he one of those homeless people?"

"He's down here on business. I told you that."

Lloyd pulled the knife from the holder. "Your momma doesn't want any more damn Yankees down here destroying the mansions." He laughed big at his own joke and then walked out, holding the knife as though dueling.

Just about exactly two-thirty, Carl's little Honda drew up at the curb. Lloyd has never understood why Carl would buy that car. He says a) it isn't pretty and b) it isn't comfortable and c) it isn't American. And Carl says d) he doesn't buy stuff to subsidize poor manufacturing even if it is American.

Lloyd went outside to greet them while Momma and I stood at the window. The man was about forty or so and he looked real spiffy. He wore a dark blue suit and a pink striped shirt with a white collar and a necktie that looked like an explosion in a jungle. His hair was shiny black with swatches of gray at his temples.

Momma said, "Look at that patent leather hair. I bet he paints it." She flounced her shoulders.

After Carl gave Momma and me our hello-kisses, he said, "Granny, Mom, this is Chalmers MacRae."

"We're delighted to see you, Mr. MacRae," Momma said, holding her hand toward the fellow, her wrist humped and her fingers drooping, as though she expected him to kiss her hand. She was playing the gracious Southern lady, and I could see Carl smiling.

"Call me Chalmers, please."

Carl said, "I don't know that you want to get that familiar with him, Granny. He's a banker, and the meanest kind of banker there is—from New York City." He leaned in to watch Momma's reaction.

"Oh, I can see that Chalmers is not mean, Carl." She cocked her head and smiled sweetly.

"I hope you haven't had bad experiences with bankers," Chalmers said.

"Foreclosed my uncle's farm in '33," she said.

"Oh, dear. Oh, my," Chalmers said. He pretended to look around wildly for a way to escape. "I guess I'm really in Dutch."

"Not at all," Momma said, waving her hand gently in the air. "We don't harbor grudges down here. If we did, we wouldn't allow any Yankees, now would we? Jean, surely you don't intend us to stand in the hall all afternoon, do you?"

I have to admit that the rhubarb pie was the prize of the dinner. The four of them finished the whole thing off, with Carl doing at least half the damage. When he had finished the last piece, he slapped his belly.

"I'd marry a woman could make a rhubarb pie like that," he said, winking at Chalmers and nodding toward Momma. I knew what he was up to, but I wasn't quick enough to stop him. "I'd marry Loretta, if she wasn't so old."

Momma didn't say a word, but she primped her lips.

Carl raised his eyebrows. "What's wrong, Granny? You think she's too skinny? I don't mind that. I like my women skinny. That's how come I favor you so much."

Momma's glare could have hammered a twopenny nail through a two-by-four, but she turned to Chalmers and smiled. "Now Chalmers," she said, "tell us all about yourself. You say you live in New York City?" Carl gave me an exasperated look.

Chalmers nodded. "Manhattan. The Big Apple."

Carl said, "Hey, Granny, didn't you say you wouldn't be caught dead up there?"

"Of course a body wants to die in his own bed," Momma said.

"You always say folks up there leave sick people out on the streets to die, just jump right over them."

"Do you think people are more charitable down here?" Chalmers asked.

Momma gave her little smug smile. "Nobody in Demopolis went hungry if the Butterfields had a cup of flour to make biscuits. And I have to admit I don't like all the drugs and pornography and such that everybody up there seems to enjoy so."

Chalmers said, "I hope you don't think I'm into anything like that."

"I don't know a thing about you except you and Carl are..." pausing "... building a tall building."

"Carl told me you were dead-set against the project," Chalmers said.

"Not at all," Momma said, widening her eyes as though nothing could be further from the truth. "If it is progress it is all right, but if it isn't it isn't." She sat back. "I guess what you're doing is progress. Folks do have to have a place to live even if it has to be way up in the air." She smiled a tight smile.

"I'm glad you approve," Carl said, "because we're going to turn Mobile into the Gulf Coast's New York and we're coming after Montgomery next."

Momma looked from Carl to Chalmers, but she just primped her lips and managed to stay quiet.

"What's the next project?" Lloyd asked.

"That's what Chalmers is down here for. The company's buying the old Woodward Gardens to build a shopping mall."

"What?" Momma cried. "Destroy all those lovely azaleas? Surely the Woodwards would never sell."

"They seem pretty eager for the money," Chalmers said.

"The New South is rising, Granny," Carl said. "Better grab a life jacket or learn to swim."

Momma shook her head, "I guess I can't criticize them too much. There's a filling station where our old family home was."

Carl shot Chalmers a look. "Our old family? I didn't know we were from an old family."

Momma glittered her eyes at Chalmers as though they were in cahoots in getting the best of Carl. "Tell me how somebody's family could not be old. You don't think we just sprang out of the dust, do you?"

We all had to laugh, none so loud as Chalmers. A little pleased expression stole over Momma's face. Then she remembered she was a gracious Southern lady and she said,

"I'm afraid Jean's neglected you, Chalmers. Can't she get you something else?"

Chalmers said he wouldn't be eating again for three days, and Carl said since it was already six o'clock they ought to head back to Mobile. We all went out to the front stoop. Carl gave me and Momma our goodbye-kisses and Lloyd a hug.

Chalmers took Momma's hand in both of his and shaking his head in a sad way said, "I hope you'll forgive me for my part in this shopping mall."

That seemed to mollify Momma a little. "Of course, I don't expect any better of you, being a Yankee, but Carl ought to be ashamed of himself for being a party to it."

"I'm not a Yankee," Chalmers said, smiling at her. "I was born in Tupelo, Mississippi."

"Mississippi?" Momma looked as though she had been pole-axed. Her mouth fell ajar and her eyes opened up to her hairline. "You're a Southerner," she said in an accusing voice.

Chalmers turned to Carl. "Didn't you tell them I was from Mississippi?"

Carl shrugged. "I don't know whether I did or not."

"You deliberately did not," Momma said. "If you had, I'd have told this boy what I really think about your New South and all this money-money-money. You knew I wouldn't discuss the subject in front of a Yankee. I guess you think you got the best of me, don't you?"

"That'll be the day, Miss Scarlett," Carl said, with a rueful laugh. He took Momma by the shoulders and gave her a hug so big she vanished.

In early April, Momma decided she wanted to see the Woodwards' azaleas one last time. I told her the mall project was years off, but she said we couldn't trust Carl, so we better go when we knew the gardens were still there. I telephoned Carl to say we were coming. He said he would go with us if we'd pick him up at his office and then let him take us to lunch.

Mobile is about three hours' driving from Montgomery, so

we set out early in the morning. The countryside was beautiful. Newly planted fields looked fresh and moist, and I could imagine beautiful green and yellow vegetables suddenly appearing on my table. I said, "Look, Momma, isn't it pretty?"

"I'll do the looking, you do the driving," she said.

The minute we pulled up in front of Carl's office, he was out the door. He is considerate that way. "Well, Granny," he said, "you're just in the nick of time." He climbed in the back and patted our shoulders to say hello. "The bulldozers are rattling down the highways." Momma did not even smile.

Woodward Gardens was located on the outskirts of town. The house was immense and had long wide galleries across the front of both floors. When the Woodwards had got rich in the shipbuilding business during the First World War, they bought the old house and planted the gardens. But just before the Second World War, the family blood seems to have gotten watery, for they sold the business to an Idaho man who turned it into one of the most prosperous shipbuilding companies in the whole country.

The money the Idaho man paid must have flowed pretty quick through the Woodwards' hands: for years they had been charging a dollar for what they used to invite folks to see free. But even though it was a business enterprise, it was still pretty. Azalea bushes a couple of yards wide and brilliant crimson and coral and white blooms flowing down the little hills, daffodils and tulips in between the azaleas, a rose garden ready to blossom off to the side, dogwood trees heavy with pink and white flowers.

As we walked along the paths, Momma was delighted. "Look at those big red azaleas," she said, nodding at them as if greeting old friends. "They must be twelve feet high."

"They are nice," Carl said, pausing in thought. "Maybe the architect could save them."

Momma gave me one of her little triumphant looks. "So you're changing your tune," she said.

Carl grinned, and I feared that from then on they would

be hard at it. We walked on down another path, me and Momma side by side and Carl bringing up the rear.

Momma paused. "Look at that cute little old statue. Wonder did the Woodwards make it at the shipyards."

"I bet if you turned it over, it would say MADE IN TAIWAN," Carl said. Momma flounced on down the path. Carl raised his eyebrows at me and looked innocent.

When we got to the pond at the back of the place, we stopped for a minute to watch the minnows scooting between the water lilies.

Momma said, "Isn't that about the prettiest thing you ever saw."

Carl said, "We're going to have a dozen fountains shooting water forty feet in the air, and little gardens all down the mall prettier than this one. You'll love it, Granny."

Momma wheeled on him, looking personally insulted. "And the azaleas will be plastic and the roses made of paper and the trees nothing but painted cement. You're going to destroy the natural beauty of this place."

"This pond's not natural," Carl said. "Manmade. Cement."

Momma hummed a moment. "But surely you won't deny that the water is natural," she finally said.

After we had passed the dogwood grove, a guide barred our way and gestured us down a little cinder path with tall pines on both sides. "You want to go see the slave quarters," he declared, with his finger pointed at us. We didn't seem to have any choice. At the back of the property we came upon a long, low unpainted frame shack with a rough-hewn sign over the door, and burned into the sign were the words "Slave Quarters." It was the gift shop.

Inside there were five tables, a soda fountain counter, and a long glass case containing replicas of the house and dolls dressed in antebellum clothes and coffee mugs and plates with drawings of the Woodward mansion on them, and in the corner dusty, three-foot copies of the statue. Carl got our drinks at the counter and brought them to us at one of the tables.

"The only thing authentically Southern about this place is the Coca-Cola," Carl said, handing us our straws.

"What do you mean?" I asked.

"This wasn't any slave quarters. I checked out the whole place before we bought it. This building isn't ten years old."

"You're just saying that to rile me," Momma said. "Why would the Woodwards pretend?"

Carl smiled innocently. "I guess they were just trying to recapture our wonderful heritage, Granny. Slavery and all that? Isn't that our heritage?"

Momma made as though to say something, apparently couldn't think of anything, and so just flounced her shoulders.

Just then two women my age and an old lady came into the gift shop. We watched as they got their Coca-Colas and sat down at the next table. The old lady wore a glittery silk dress and short fur jacket, but her white hair had a touch too much blue in it. The youngish ones wore silk suits and bright blouses. One was hawk-faced and the other round-headed exactly like the old lady.

I could almost see Momma's ear telescoping out to hear what they were saying. She didn't need to stretch much—they were talking the way people do when they want to be overheard. The hawk-faced woman said her granddaddy had gone to Sewanee with one of the Woodwards and had spent a night in the house. Her tone suggested that was worth at least a medal. The old lady tried to top it by saying she herself had been in the house with a group that had visited all the old mansions between Pensacola and Biloxi.

Momma cannot resist making friends. She bumped her chair around toward the old lady and said, "Have you ever seen such lovely flowers?"

The old lady rocked her chair a little closer to Momma's until their knees were almost touching, and said she never had. That broke the ice. We told each other where we were from—they were from Jacksonville, Florida, and were staying overnight at Point Clear—and who we knew in the other's home town. I knew somebody in Jacksonville they had heard of, and the hawk-faced woman had a distant cousin in Montgomery who went to my church. We all smiled and felt comfortable. Carl could hardly keep from laughing.

Then the hawk-faced woman said, "I hear they're tearing this lovely place down to make a shopping mall."

"Isn't it a shame?" the daughter said.

Momma gave Carl a pleased look. "I couldn't agree more."

Carl winked at me and scrunched his face, pretending he was embarrassed and frightened.

"It makes me feel sick at my stomach," the old lady said. She leaned over and hugged her middle to prove the point. The daughter patted her mother on the back.

The hawk-faced woman said, "Makes me sick, too, but not physically." Her face soured as though that wouldn't be true for long.

The old lady straightened up. "Why on earth would a nice family like the Woodwards do such a thing?"

Carl made his eyes wide and innocent. "You reckon maybe they couldn't make a living selling Coca-Colas and dolls?"

Momma primped her lips and shook her head. "Now, hush."

"Wonder how much they got for it?" the daughter asked.

"Quite a bundle," Carl said.

Momma said, "I think I know somebody else in Jacksonville."

The daughter clucked and shook her head. "Some sly Yankee probably hoodwinked the Woodwards into it."

"No," Carl said. "The buyers are one-hundred percent Southern."

Momma took a suck on her straw so hard it's a wonder the bottom of the paper cup didn't pull out.

"Young man," said the old lady, "you seem to like the idea

of destroying these gardens."

"As a matter of fact," Carl began.

Momma said, "Carl, will you go get the car? I'm kind of tired."

"But I haven't finished my drink," he said, grinning at her.

I jingled the car keys at him. "Get the car." Carl was laughing, but he stood up and took the keys. It's funny that a mother can order a child around long after the child is ordering other folks around.

The hawk-faced woman said, "I can understand a Yankee doing such a thing, but never a Southerner."

Momma looked uncomfortable for a minute. Then she said, "If the Yankees are going to do it anyway, isn't it better to keep the money down here?"

"And contribute to the destruction of our heritage?"

"Our heritage?" Momma chewed on that a minute. "I'd much rather see a shopping mall with pretty gardens and fountains than slave quarters any day, even phony ones."

The old lady sniffed. "Well, I don't believe any Southerner with background and family should be a party to destroying the Old South this way."

That was it. Momma rose up as tall as she could and glared down her face at the old lady. "My grandson is a very distinguished businessman from a very old and proud Southern family. I hope you enjoy your stay."

She nodded to them and turned away. As I followed her out of the shack, I heard the old lady say, "What was that about her grandson?" and the daughter said, "I didn't quite catch it."

We walked back down the path. When we got near the front gate where Carl was waiting with the car, Momma stopped and pulled me around by my arm. "Now, Jean," she said, poking her finger in my chest, "it wouldn't be fair for you to tell Carl what I said back there."

I said I wouldn't mention it.

Vím

LLOYD's brother-in-law's uncle Franklin Epp stopped in Montgomery on his way from Minneapolis to spend the winter in Florida. He had been an Alabama boy himself once upon a time, but he had gone north to make his fortune. Lloyd's sister Estelle hinted it was quite a fortune. He had invented a newfangled glue you could not get loose unless you boiled it in some funny chemical Mr. Epp had also invented. She said he got one-third of a penny for every bottle sold.

"I don't believe a word of it," Momma said when we told her.

"Estelle doesn't fib, Mrs. Blaine," Lloyd said.

"Did I say she fibbed?" Momma asked, primping her mouth at him. "I said she was misinformed, and heaven knows that has happened often enough."

She turned and winked at me. She does love to tease Lloyd. But this time he didn't rise to it. He just scraped the sole of his shoe against the glass top of the coffee table. I closed my eyes so I wouldn't see the particles of grime floating down to the blue rug.

"You didn't know Franklin Epp and I were schoolmates back in Demopolis, now did you, Lloyd?"

Lloyd said, "No'm."

"Well, we were. That scrawny-necked boy could not have grown up to be a man of money. I don't mean to hurt your feelings, since you are nearly kin to him, but he was a dunce."

I decided to take Lloyd's part. "They thought Einstein was a dunce. See how wrong they were."

"Now, Jean, did Einstein ever claim he invented glue?" Momma tossed her head to show she had gotten the best of the argument.

When Mr. Epp had been in town two days, Estelle and Eddie invited the three of us for dinner. They live in a trailer park on the edge of town. They have enough money to live in a real house—four years ago, Eddie sold his grocery store in Andalusia to Dixie Duzzit Rite Supermarkets for a lot of money—but they claimed owning real estate would tie them down, and Eddie is dead set on traveling. Every spring they go to a different state. Momma asked Lloyd if so much traveling meant they didn't like their family. That time Lloyd rose to the occasion and said, "Just wait a minute, Mrs. Blaine, just wait a minute."

When Momma gave him a sweet, waiting smile, he subsided.

When we drove up to the trailer, we could see at once that the money part about Mr. Epp must have been right, for parked next to Eddie's Buick was a tiny foreign-looking red convertible. Lloyd whistled and said it must have cost forty-fifty thousand dollars.

"How many tubes of glue you reckon that is?" Momma asked. Lloyd reached for the little stub of a pencil and the notebook he keeps on top of the sunshade. About once a day he forgets and jerks down the sunshade and gets hit in the face.

"Never mind," I said, for just then the trailer door flew open and an old man came down the steps. His bent knees were so stiff he didn't walk so much as rock from side to side, like a daddy-longlegs bug. He was just beginning to have that shiny, tight old man skin, and his hair was as pale and soft as a newborn chick. At least he had a good chin, which was more than you could say for the general run of Epp. Eddie's chin receded so bad Momma said you had to wonder what his bottom teeth rested on.

"Clara," Mr. Epp shouted. "Long time no see, but I'd've recognized you in Timbuktu."

"Fibber," Momma whispered. "I'm bound to have changed some in fifty years."

When she got out of the car, Mr. Epp grabbed her around the shoulders and gave her a big kiss right on the lips. Momma wiped her hand across her mouth and then down the side of her dress. She drew herself up and rared back, staring at Mr. Epp. "I know you are related to Eddie and Eddie is related to Lloyd and Lloyd is related to Jean, but I would not have thought you and I were kissing kin."

"Get modern, Clara," Mr. Epp cried, throwing his hands skyward as if leading a cheer. "Everybody kisses these days. It's the in-thing to do."

"Everybody may kiss, but I do not kiss everybody," Momma said.

Mr. Epp seemed to think that was about the funniest thing he had ever heard. He commenced to laugh and snort and gasp and choke. Lloyd pounded him on the back and set him down on the trailer steps. He sat there panting and grinning at Momma.

When he finally caught his breath, he said, "You didn't use to be so particular, Clara Butterfield. Remember playing post office and spin the bottle?"

Momma lifted her face up and away from him. "I have no idea what you are talking about."

Lloyd said, "Sure you do, Mrs. Blaine. You sit around in a circle? And spin a quart-size milk bottle? And kiss who it points at?"

Momma said, "I don't believe I asked for an explanation, Lloyd."

From his perch on the steps, Mr. Epp kept on grinning at Momma. "And a few other times, too, when there wasn't a crowd. You had the prettiest, softest little rosebud lips I just about ever kissed."

"Franklin, you are still a dunce," Momma said as she stalked past him into the trailer.

Mr. Epp began to laugh again and choke again, and Lloyd had to pound him again. When he recovered, Mr. Epp said, "She's as full of vim as ever, ain't she?"

While we waited for dinner, Mr. Epp told us his plans just as though we had asked. He said this year he might not stay a full winter at his place on Key Biscayne because he'd like to travel, and he had picked the island of Mykonos in Greece as his destination. He said he had never been there, but he had heard it was about as pretty as the Florida Keys.

Momma said, "If they're about the same, Franklin, why not stay home and save your money?"

"I like adventure," he answered. "Keeps the blood flowing. Haven't you ever wanted to travel?"

"I'm quite happy with my own home," Momma said. She pursed her lips. "Even if it isn't my own home."

Sometimes I think she talked like that just to get a rise out of me—and she never failed. Lloyd thought she did it to get reassurance that she was wanted. But I couldn't imagine she needed more reassurance than she got every single day. "It is so your home," I said. "It wouldn't be a home without you."

"But I don't hold the mortgage," she said, flicking her fingers as though shaking water off them.

Mr. Epp said, "I had my daughter and son-in-law come live with me, but when they were out I wished they'd come home and when they were home I wished they'd go out."

"Mine take me out with them if I want to go," Momma said.

"We don't even like to go without her," I said.

Mr. Epp laughed again, but not dangerously this time. "But, Clara, when there was the flood, Noah had the folks go in two by two, not in threes."

"I'm glad I wasn't on the water, twos or threes," Momma said. "I'd get seasick."

"Have you ever been on an ocean voyage?" Eddie asked.

"No," Momma admitted, "but the ocean is just a big lake, and I been on a lake and didn't like it a bit." Mr. Epp cackled and gasped and choked again.

That little trailer home is a miracle. Estelle can pull out this and push in that and twist something else and seat six people where you didn't even know there was a table. She claimed the best thing about the trailer was that the pushing and the pulling did all the dusting the place ever needed.

She served us Cornish hens baked in orange juice, sesame seeds, and honey—she said she had eaten that in Vermont in the spring. Every year we had to eat some peculiar concoction Eddie and Estelle brought home from their travels. Last year they brought back something from Utah that was so hard to chew Momma said the main ingredient had to be pig toenails.

When Momma took a bite of the Cornish, she shot me a quick look indicating nausea, and then she smiled at Estelle. "This dish is mighty tasty, but don't you think a little pepper would cut the sweet in a nice way?"

Mr. Epp slapped his hands together. "Why, Clara, that's just you to perfection," he cried. "You were always a little pepper cutting the sweet in a nice way." He was sitting opposite Momma, and he leaned across at her and made a little kissing sound. Momma sat up straight and stared across the table

I rushed in. "Eddie, where're y'all going this coming spring?"

That was a lucky stroke. It set him and Estelle off talking about New Mexico, carrying us right through salad and into dessert. And then Mr. Epp said, "I bet they don't have naked bathing in New Mexico the way they do in Mykonos."

Momma does not like anything suggestive. She will not attend a movie where men and women are naked in bed, and

she will not let anybody but Lloyd tell her a dirty joke. So I
was not surprised when she stood up and said, "Jean, that
headache I told you about has come back. You better take me
home."

Mr. Epp protested vigorously, occasionally gasping and
choking, but when it was clear Momma was standing her
ground, he insisted on holding her elbow all the way down the
steps and to the car. Once she was seated, he lifted her coat
collar up around her neck. When he tucked the edge of her
skirt under her leg, Momma slapped his hand.

"I can take care of my own garments," she said, and at
that Mr. Epp laughed so much Eddie had to half-carry him
back up the steps.

The next morning at nine-thirty there came a huge bouquet of
American Beauty roses for Momma. Momma said, "I suppose
that dunce has sent an armload of posies to every widow in
town, just showing off his money." After she read the card,
she handed it to me, saying, "Can't even spell."

It was a pretty little card with a picture of flowers in the
corner. On it was written in a spidery hand, "Hope your
headahce's vanished in time for a visit this aft at 3."

"Puff," Momma said. "I have more important things to do,"

At three, Momma was in the living room, embroidering a
pillow case. When we heard Mr. Epp's little roadster scraping
the curb, she went over to the settee to see out the window.
She said, "That's a silly car for a man who can't bend his
knees." I looked out. Mr. Epp was twisted around on the seat
and lifting his legs out of the car with both hands, as though
they were logs.

I answered the doorbell and led Mr. Epp into the living
room. Casting no more than a glance at him, Momma said,
"Thank you for the flowers. They are pretty." She motioned at
the corner table where I had them in my best cut-glass vase.

Without bothering to look at the flowers, Mr. Epp just
went straight over to Momma and kissed the top of her head.

"Lovely flowers for a lovely lady," he said. "My, you look pretty."

"Have a seat," was all Momma could think to say. She motioned at a chair across the room, but Mr. Epp set himself down right beside her on the settee.

He hitched around so he could see her face better.

"Clara Butterfield," he said in a musing tone. "Sweet little Clara Butterfield. It's a marvel, us meeting after all these years."

"Nothing strange about it at all, Franklin," Momma said. "Our kin married, you came to see yours, they invited mine over, and that's that."

"No," he said, shaking his head, "it's destiny." He turned to me and sighed. "I liked your momma a mighty lot in the old days, but I was too poor to say a word." He reached over and took Momma's hand off the embroidery frame. "I would've put a ring on this very finger if I'd've had a dollar to buy it with."

"You wouldn't have any such thing." Momma jerked her hand back. "Surely I would have had something to say about it."

Mr. Epp pretended to look outraged. "You're not supposed to talk to rich men that way, Clara. Show some respect for all my money."

"I have my carfare," Momma said.

"Oh, she's such a spitfire," he said. That made him start coughing and gasping and choking. Momma tried to hide her smile, but I could tell she was pleased with herself.

Once Mr. Epp calmed down, he began asking about people they had known when they were young. Momma told how this one drank so much they couldn't even find his liver when he died and that one sold her farm six months before they discovered oil on it and the other's granddaughter was Miss Alabama in Atlantic City though she was uglier than burnt turnips. Mr. Epp laughed so hard I was afraid he would choke to death.

It is only polite when friends and kin entertain folks from out of town that you help out by inviting everybody to take a meal. So the next night it was our turn to put on dinner for Eddie and Estelle and Mr. Epp. That time both Momma and I got an armload of roses.

"Isn't he nice," I said.

Momma said, "Doesn't he know Lloyd grows the best roses in the world?"

"But they don't bloom in November."

"Surely, Jean, you don't think people ought to have roses blooming in November. It's against nature."

Mr. Epp brought us a half-gallon bottle of glue as a house gift. Lloyd was so excited I was afraid he was going to break something just to glue it back together. He said, "We been using staplers to make the pup tents because the glues just don't hold to the posts. But I'm wondering if this stuff mightn't be better."

When Mr. Epp saw Momma sitting in the rocker, he cried, "Aren't you going to sit on the settee beside me?"

"If you want company on the settee, ask Eddie."

"Eddie won't let me hold his hand."

"Nor will I," Momma said. "You can keep your Roman hands and Russian fingers to yourself." She had a little pleased smirk on her face.

Mr. Epp went through his routine, laughing, snorting, choking. Eddie pushed him down on the settee and began banging him on the back. "See what I mean, Eddie," Mr. Epp gasped. "Still full of vim."

Lloyd said, "It would seal the air spaces in the short run, but I wonder if it would hold as well as staples."

"Now, Lloyd," I said, "we don't discuss business at a social gathering."

Mr. Epp said, "If we talk about glue, you can take the dinner off your income tax. I took seventeen thousand dollars worth of dinners off mine last year. I figured I never ate I didn't at least mention glue."

"You're lucky the government didn't throw you in jail," Momma said.

"That's what you got smart lawyers and accountants for, Clara. Of course, I had to pay them seventeen thousand dollars to get the seventeen thousand off."

Momma had to laugh in spite of herself.

Toward the end of dinner, Mr. Epp took over the talking. He told about his wife who was dead fifteen months. He said she had been a good wife and he had been a good husband—no hanky panky either way, faithful as old dog Tray, he said. It was right after she passed that he had tried living with his daughter.

"Now I'm looking for a new companion," he went on. "I'm too young and Minneapolis is too cold for me to sleep by myself. I got plenty of money and I still got plenty of vim. Quite a few ladies will attest to that if you don't believe me."

Momma looked at Mr. Epp as if he had a contagious skin disease.

I jumped up and said, "Anybody want any more pecan pie?" Whenever you ask people if they want any more and they don't, they know it's time to go home.

After they had left, Momma sat down on the settee and shook her head. "I've never been so shocked in all my life."

"What did he do that was so bad this time?" Lloyd asked.

"Bragging about his 'vim.'"

"That's not a dirty word, is it, Mrs. Blaine?" Lloyd asked.

"The way he said it it was. He's just a dirty old man. Men get that way. Nothing personal, Lloyd."

The next morning came more roses, and the next afternoon at three o'clock came Mr. Epp. When the doorbell rang, Momma drew back the curtain and looked out the window. "It's Franklin Epp," she said.

"Don't worry. We just won't answer the door."

"I didn't raise you to be rude to Lloyd's people," she said.

Mr. Epp wouldn't let me take his coat—actually a maroon leather jacket. He said he wanted to take Momma for a ride in his little red car. Momma said she didn't want to go riding. Mr. Epp said in that case I could take his coat and he would spend the afternoon there. Then Momma said she would go for a ride if I would.

"This car's like the ark, Clara," Mr. Epp said. "There ain't room but for two." He winked at me.

"You go then, Jean," Momma said.

"But I don't want Jean—I want *you*," he said. He pointed at her as though he was Uncle Sam in the recruiting poster from the war. "You aren't afraid of me, are you, Clara?"

Momma flounced her shoulders. "I'm not afraid of the devil himself, but I don't necessarily want to spend the afternoon with him."

Mr. Epp began to laugh. I thought he was going to have another one of his fits, so I pounded him on the back to ward it off. I said, "You won't be gone long, Momma."

She gave me a look that would have fried eggs, but she went.

I thought they would take just a little spin, but they weren't home after two hours. I thought accident. I thought kidnapping a rich man. I thought stroke and heart attack out on a country road. I called Estelle and Eddie but they weren't home. I called Lloyd, and he said give them until six o'clock and then he'd call the Alabama Highway Patrol.

That is just exactly how long they took. Momma did not even apologize, though I didn't hide that I'd been frantic. She said they had been to Demopolis and drunk a Coca-Cola at a cafe where the old feed store used to be. They had driven out to the old Epp place on the edge of town and found nothing but a broken-down barn and a shed over the well. She already knew her folks's old place had turned into a gas station.

After dinner, we went into the den to watch television. In

the middle of a shoot-out, Momma said, "He's kind of cute."

I said, "The man with the gun or the one down in the alley?"

Lloyd said, "She means Mr. Epp. Now y'all be quiet so we can hear the show."

Mr. Epp sent roses each of the next three mornings. I was so tired of roses that I just put the last batch in an old tin mop bucket. Every day at three on the dot, Mr. Epp showed up to take Momma riding. One day it was Auburn, the next day, Troy, and then Andalusia. In the evening when we watched the television, Momma sat there making her usual remarks at the screen—saying this one was a fool and that one was a hussy—but they didn't sound right. It was as though she was trying to be the same as she always was but couldn't quite get in the rhythm of it.

Finally I couldn't contain myself any longer. I said, "All this traipsing around is just wearing you out. We'll put a stop to it if that old fool is bothering you."

I expected one of her flouncy answers. but all she said was, "No need."

She stood up and went off to her room. I remoted off the television so I could get Lloyd's undivided attention. I said, "Momma is sure acting funny, as though she has something on her mind."

Lloyd laughed. "She's got courting on her mind."

There it was, out in the open. I felt my heart begin to pound. It was wrong for a stranger to come in and try to break us up. And Lloyd just sitting there doing nothing. "So," I said, "you want him to take Momma away from us."

"Did I say that? Funny, I didn't hear myself say that."

"Then why are you siding with Mr. Epp against me?"

"Don't be jealous, Jean. Nothing'll come of it. Let them have a little fun." He reached over and took the machine from my hand and remoted the television back on. He can be very exasperating when he deliberately fails to get the point.

∾

Mr. Epp was supposed to leave on Saturday, and on Friday he came to take Momma out to dinner. I tried to get them to eat with us, but he wouldn't hear of it. I thought he'd be polite enough to ask us to eat with them, but he ignored my hints. There wasn't anything I could do but wait.

He brought her home about nine-thirty, and she came into the den and watched the last half hour of television. As usual, at ten o'clock Lloyd yawned and said, "Beddybyes."

Momma said, "Jean, let's have a heart-to-heart."

I jumped up and banged my shin against the coffee table and fell back to the couch. Lloyd gave us both a look, but he recognized this was ladies only, and he went upstairs without another word. I was afraid to speak. Momma got out of her rocker and came over to sit beside me on the couch. She cocked up on her hip so she could look right into my eyes. She said, "Jean, Franklin has invited me to go with him to that Greek island."

I laughed to show her it was just a joke. "I can't picture you lying out naked on the beach with all the other naked people."

She slapped that away. "I wouldn't have to lie on the beach naked or otherwise, Jean. That is not the point."

I knew I had to be careful. Momma can be ornery. If she thinks you are trying to run her, she will do what you don't want her to even if she wouldn't have wanted to do it if she hadn't thought you didn't want her to. I felt as though I was walking barefoot through a briar patch.

"So Mr. Epp wants you to marry him," I said, biding my time.

"Don't be such a stick-in-the-mud," she said. "Franklin says it's best to test if you get along before you go legal. It's the in-thing. I know traveling with him would be fun. I haven't had so much fun in years."

I would have had to be made of stone not to feel that like a mallet to my head. I had been so proud when she had decided to live with us that I did everything I could to make her happy. I had even gone with her halfway across the country to visit my brother Thad though I had not anticipated a speck of pleasure in it. And I had sometimes neglected Lloyd to take her to the movies or to a ladies' club meeting, and all Lloyd ever said was, Have a good time.

"You don't have fun with us?" I asked her.

"I didn't say I didn't," she said, twisting impatiently. "You are just too dag sensitive. What I said was not as much. Franklin makes me laugh. It was all I could do over in Auburn to keep him from buying me a little red car twin to his. The salesman thought we were lunatics."

"If it's a car you want," I said, "Lloyd will buy you one."

"If I wanted a car, I would buy one for myself, Jean. You know I like to be chauffeured so I can see the road better."

"Well, what is it, then? If there's something I've done or haven't done or Lloyd has or hasn't, all you have to do is tell us."

She smiled. "Though I know it will hurt your feelings to hear it," she said, "it's not you I'm worrying about." She turned so I couldn't see her face and she spoke into her own shoulder. "I'll be honest with you, Jean: I'm out of the habit of thinking about this…this vim business."

Suddenly I saw a picture of Momma and Mr. Epp that I did not like. I said, "That dirty old man. You said so yourself."

She looked at me as though I had told a horrible lie. "I never said it," she said. "And if I did I was just teasing. It's perfectly normal and healthy to care about all that." She paused and looked down at her hands. "But I'm scared. I've been a widow nearly six years and might as well have been nine years before that when your father was so sick." She snuck a look at me. "I'm just not used to thinking along those lines."

I said, "You don't have to fool with all that anymore, Momma. It's behind you now."

"I've just gotten so old and droopy," she said, touching her breasts, "and my skin is just like a plucked chicken left out in the sun, and, well, there's lots else that happens you'll find out for yourself soon enough. I might be too ashamed." Then she laughed. "But I bet Franklin's no Rudolph Valentino—maybe we could just be ashamed together."

I was so agitated I was ready to bite my elbows, but I was able to hold on. I said, "Momma, you don't have to do anything you don't want to do. Nobody can make you."

"Thing is, what do I want to do?" She looked away from me and laughed in an embarrassed way. "Maybe I'd hate it, though I didn't use to hate it." Her cheeks pinkened. "Franklin says we'll take our time with all that until I'm ready."

We hadn't talked about all that since the night before Lloyd and I married, and then all she had said was for me not to worry. I said, "I can't believe we're having this conversation."

"No point stopping now—we're coming to the end. Jean, since your father died, Franklin is the first man except Lloyd to buy me so much as a Co-Cola. First man to send me flowers. First man to say I was pretty. First to put his arms around me and kiss me."

I said, "And you actually let him? Did you like it?"

"I sure liked the idea he wanted to do it."

I held her gaze with mine. "Aren't you happy with us?"

"I'm content," she said. "But don't you think maybe there could be more than just content?"

Her shy little smile nearly broke my heart. And I thought maybe she could have more than just contentment. I knew I had to set aside my own hurt. "Well," I said, "I guess it's only sensible for you to find out."

I took her in my arms. She felt like a tiny rag-doll child, so soft and frail. "Thank you, Jean," she said, her voice muffled against my shoulder. "I told Franklin I wouldn't do it unless you were for it."

I had to laugh at that. Then my eyes welled up, for though

I tightened my hold, I could already feel her slipping away from me. We gave each other a kiss, and she went into her room and I up to mine.

Lloyd was sound asleep. As I put on my nightgown in the dark, I willed myself to imagine Momma and Mr. Epp walking on the beach at Mykonos, grinning at the naked folks. Momma whispered something funny, and the two of them got to laughing. Mr. Epp commenced to choke and gasp, and Momma whacked him on his back. Then I saw him give her a kiss on the lips, right there in front of everybody.

I got in bed. Lloyd has the nicest warm back in the world, and I hugged him tight. I whispered, "Now it's just you and me. Two by two." I didn't know whether I was happy or sad.